Case's Adam's apple pumped up and down. "What I'm telling you, Slocum, is that Gans LeFort has brothers. Six of them. Six brothers! Plus himself! And each one is as tough and as miserable and vicious as the next."

Slocum had walked to the door. With his hand on the knob he turned, nodded, adjusted his Stetson hat a little more forward on his head. "Good to know I got something to look forward to."

OTHER BOOKS BY JAKE LOGAN

RIDE, SLOCUM, RIDE
HANGING JUSTICE
SLOCUM AND THE WIDOW KATE
ACROSS THE RIO GRANDE
THE COMANCHE'S WOMAN
SLOCUM'S GOLD
BLOODY TRAIL TO TEXAS
NORTH TO DAKOTA
SLOCUM'S WOMAN
WHITE HELL
RIDE FOR REVENGE
OUTLAW BLOOD
MONTANA SHOWDOWN
SEE TEXAS AND DIE
IRON MUSTANG
SHOTGUNS FROM HELL
SLOCUM'S BLOOD
SLOCUM'S FIRE
SLOCUM'S REVENGE
SLOCUM'S HELL
SLOCUM'S GRAVE
DEAD MAN'S HAND
FIGHTING VENGEANCE
SLOCUM'S SLAUGHTER
ROUGHRIDER
SLOCUM'S RAGE
HELLFIRE
SLOCUM'S CODE
SLOCUM'S FLAG
SLOCUM'S RAID
SLOCUM'S RUN
BLAZING GUNS
SLOCUM'S GAMBLE
SLOCUM'S DEBT
SLOCUM AND THE MAD MAJOR
THE NECKTIE PARTY
THE CANYON BUNCH
SWAMP FOXES
LAW COMES TO COLD RAIN
SLOCUM'S DRIVE
JACKSON HOLE TROUBLE
SILVER CITY SHOOTOUT
SLOCUM AND THE LAW
APACHE SUNRISE
SLOCUM'S JUSTICE
NEBRASKA BURNOUT
SLOCUM AND THE CATTLE QUEEN
SLOCUM'S WOMEN
SLOCUM'S COMMAND
SLOCUM GETS EVEN
SLOCUM AND THE LOST DUTCHMAN MINE
HIGH COUNTRY HOLDUP
GUNS OF SOUTH PASS
SLOCUM AND THE HATCHET MEN
BANDIT GOLD
SOUTH OF THE BORDER
DALLAS MADAM
TEXAS SHOWDOWN
SLOCUM IN DEADWOOD
SLOCUM'S WINNING HAND
SLOCUM AND THE GUN RUNNERS
SLOCUM'S PRIDE
SLOCUM'S CRIME
THE NEVADA SWINDLE
SLOCUM'S GOOD DEED

JAKE LOGAN
SLOCUM'S STAMPEDE

BERKLEY BOOKS, NEW YORK

SLOCUM'S STAMPEDE

A Berkley Book/published by arrangement with
the author

PRINTING HISTORY
Berkley edition/April 1985

All rights reserved.
Copyright © 1985 by Jake Logan.
This book may not be reproduced in whole or in part,
by mimeograph or any other means, without permission.
For information address: The Berkley Publishing Group,
200 Madison Avenue, New York, N.Y. 10016.

ISBN: 0-425-07654-7

A BERKLEY BOOK® TM 757,375
Berkley Books are published by The Berkley Publishing Group,
200 Madison Avenue, New York, N.Y. 10016.
The name "BERKLEY" and the stylized "B" with design are trademarks
belonging to Berkley Publishing Corporation.

PRINTED IN THE UNITED STATES OF AMERICA

1

"I'll get you, Slocum! I will get you if it's by God the last thing I do on this earth!"

"If you do get me, mister, it surely *will* be the last thing you do on this earth!"

The man lying on the floor had shot his rage at Slocum's broad back as he turned away, but the tall man with the big shoulders and thick, raven-black hair still had his eyes on him through the cracked mirror in back of the bar. Big Gans LeFort was almost immobile on the floor of the Suddenly Riches Saloon, his face and beard covered with blood, his nose broken, his right ear already thickened and turning black from John Slocum's hammering fists. Only his fury now held any real force.

Slocum moved slowly toward the batwing doors, still watching the downed man and the ring of frozen onlookers in the big gold-framed mirror. He had not escaped damage himself. His right hand, staying close to his holstered sixgun, was swollen and bloody. He knew he'd have trouble if he had to draw. But for the moment the crowd was stalled. No one had seen anything like the whipping of Gans LeFort. Nobody had ever beaten Big Gans. It had taken a while and the battle had wrecked much of the saloon, including the banisters that led to the girls' cribs along the balcony above.

Still down, Gans LeFort was trying hopelessly to raise himself, his breath sobbing out his curses. No one moved to help him; their immobility offered unmistakable tribute to John Slocum's fists. In that airless room with the low ceiling, full of tobacco smoke and the stench of sweat, nobody wished to draw the attention of the man walking toward the batwing doors, the man who had just beaten Gans LeFort to a pulp.

Slocum moved more quickly now, yet still with the care and caution of a mountain cat. In the mirror he saw the girl up on the balcony, her long blond hair falling loosely to the shoulders of her robe, which she had hastily pulled over her nakedness when LeFort had burst into the room. Exhausted as Slocum was, with his body aching from LeFort's thunderous fists, knees, and boots, he yet felt his desire rising again. But he forced his attention to the men in the room behind him, saw that no one approached the fallen man, no one offered a weapon.

He felt her watching him, knew he could have gone right back upstairs and continued where he'd left off when that big, loudmouthed, possessive son of a bitch had come charging into the room right out of nowhere and yanked him off the girl; though, thank God, they'd just finished. And for an instant he thought to climb back up to the balcony and go for seconds.

But Slocum knew better than to stretch it. Gans LeFort would have friends, men who would side with him; it would be only moments before the news had fired all through town. Slocum, on the other hand, was alone; he always had been. And he had business, besides. The girl would have to wait. Or there would be others. He didn't even remember her name... Callie, was it? But there was Eli Case. And Slocum needed the money.

Within an hour following the excitement in the Suddenly Riches Saloon he had cleaned himself up at the town's barber and bath shop and was listening to Eli J. Case in his office.

"I aim to make this the first cattle shipping point of the whole, entire American West," the cattle shipper declared, his thin lips working the words energetically around the big cigar he had clamped between his teeth. His small, intense face carried a thin mustache and a trim goatee.

Eli Case—short, pin-shouldered, chomping on his unlighted Havana. Slocum wondered whether the little man's sleeve garters were supporting his shirtsleeves or his toothpick arms. Eli was built like a spider, but he had the strength and will of a mountain lion, the memory of an elephant, and the forgiving nature of a grizzly. Slocum had heard a lot about Eli Case.

"'Course, the LeFort boys are pulling every goddamn thing they can think of to get the herds to come to New Orleans. Since the cotton went bust in the War they're figurin' to build even bigger now with beef." Case's almond eyes glittered as he leaned back in his swivel chair and regarded John Slocum.

"What do you want with me then?" And Slocum added, "I can be expensive."

Eli Case leaned forward, his little elbows carefully touching the top of the desk like two needles. His Adam's apple pumped twice in his skinny throat. He was a man who would look forty for a long time. "I know you, Slocum. I heard of you, checked on you." He said those words with the big cigar now in his hand, stabbing it, like a schoolteacher making a point with his pencil. "The LeForts have already stopped half a dozen herds from getting up into Kansas. But the Texans have kept trying even so. Them that are still alive rue it." He ran the pale tip of his tongue along his upper lip.

"So why don't they ship with the LeForts? New Orleans is a whole lot closer than Kansas." Slocum knew the answer to that, but he wanted to hear what Case had to say.

The little man's lips pursed, his eyes squeezed shut, then opened and grew big and round. He put the cigar in his mouth, and took it out again. "They were doing that; that is, before the railroad come to Abilene. At two dollars a head. And that made 'em madder'n a cat with vinegar up its ass."

"Nobody's getting rich on that kind of money."

"I am offering ten to fifteen. Full market price."

"More like it," Slocum agreed.

"There is a herd starting north from San Antone directly now." Case dropped both forearms onto the desk. "Slocum, I can't bankroll this operation much longer. But hell, man, we got everything for those cows at the shipping point—lots of water, lush bluestem grass; you've seen it, like a green carpet in those hills!" He waved the cigar. "You can't find better feed for those beeves to fatten on before shipping 'em East!"

"Excepting there's the LeForts between here and there."

"The LeForts, plus an army of gunmen." The shipper stood up suddenly and walked around the desk to stand in front of Slocum, who remained seated. "Slocum, this herd has got to get through."

"You want me to ramrod it."

Eli Case nodded once and put the unlighted cigar back in his mouth. He struck a lucifer and puffed while Slocum watched him.

"The KC herd is owned by Otis Dinwiddie. A good man, Otis, but he ain't young, and the LeForts have just got too much in advantage tools."

Slocum said nothing; there was nothing to say.

"Let me say it once again, Slocum. The KC herd has got to get through. I mean, I *need* that herd. You understand? I don't care how you do it." He paused, and in a new voice said, "I have been taking losses."

Knowing the kind of man Eli Case was, Slocum appreciated the admission.

The cattle dealer had been standing in the shadow of the room and now, as he walked back to his chair and sat down, the sunlight followed him. "I don't care how you do it," he repeated. "But the herd has got to reach Abilene by the first of May."

Slocum heard the iron ringing in those words.

"Pay me enough," he said quietly, "and it will."

"Name your figure."

Slocum told him.

Case nodded, and both men stood.

"Maybe I ought to tell you some about the LeFort boys," the cattle dealer said.

"Like Gans LeFort setting fire to a fifteen-year-old boy for spooking his horse?"

"You're still in?"

"Didn't I just say so?"

For the first time during the meeting, Eli Case seemed thrown. But he recovered swiftly. The flush that had slipped into his face left and he was again cool, deliberate, pale in those areas that were free of hair.

"I just met Gans," Slocum said.

Something almost like a rueful smile took over Case's countenance. "I heard it, and you look it."

"You could take a look at Gans LeFort," Slocum said laconically.

"I heard that, too." The smile vanished and Case's Adam's apple pumped once. "What I am telling you,

Slocum, is that Gans LeFort has brothers. Six of them. Six brothers! Plus himself! And each one is just as tough and miserable and vicious as the next."

Slocum had walked to the door. With his hand on the knob he turned, nodded, adjusted his Stetson hat a little more forward on his head. "Good to know I got something to look forward to, then."

2

About halfway through the forenoon the weather began to fair off and Slocum drew rein, shifting his weight in the old stock saddle, as the sunlight flooded the freshened land. He felt its warmth on his hands while he lit a quirly and watched the steam rising from the spotted pony's damp withers. The horse whiffled, stuck out his right foreleg, and rubbed his long nose against it, then started to crop the short buffalo grass. Slocum studied the area for sign.

When he saw the prints of unshod horses his mouth tightened and he kicked the spotted pony forward. Of course, being so close to Indian country, such sign was to be expected; but it looked like a large party. Hunting? They were heading west, not in his direction. All to the good. But as he rode, he did not relax his vigilance.

Now the whole day heated up. By noon the land was again dry as powder and the sun had become a burning white disc in the high, pale sky. When he reached the creek in the late afternoon he walked the horse out to where the water ran well over its hocks and waited while the animal drank and rested its legs.

Slocum waited. He knew how. A jay called from a nearby cottonwood tree and rose in flight. The spotted pony suddenly lifted his head, his ears straight forward and up as he joined his rider's listening.

Slocum heard it. It was more a feeling really, an

awareness; that special premonition of danger that more than a few times had saved him in a tight spot. He had long ago learned to trust it. And from habit he was already checking his weapons, the .31 Navy Colt with the hammer-thong in its cross-draw holster, the seven-shot Henry repeater rifle in the saddle scabbard behind his knee.

His green eyes scanned the tawny land as he keened his whole body, sniffing the air, feeling the vibration of the life around him. Nothing audible came to him, only a strange stillness within the humming land, a tension, a taut waiting in the dry air. He realized what it was; it was the change of tempo. And now he became aware of a tremor in the ground.

He stood in his stirrups, his eyes soft for better vision as they swept the distance and middle ground. His tall, lean, muscular body was motionless above the horse and saddle, his buckskins caked with dust and sweat, his tanned face bone-hard from the wind and the sun and the loneliness of many trails. An alien man, yet a man who clearly was more a part of nature than most; a man close to himself, one of those rare ones whom people had to deal with on his own terms.

He sat back in the saddle and looked down at the creek water, blinking, widening and narrowing his eyes, moving his face about to make it loose. Then, with his eyes and face softer, he looked again at the horizon the way the old Cherokee had taught him long ago to look twice.

And there! The faint plume of dust rising almost at the horizon; there at the big butte. He waited, moving the pony across the creek and into the stand of cottonwoods. The plume of dust was only a spot at first, but now as it came nearer it grew long and narrow, rising out of the sun-baked earth, enveloping everything under it, coming slowly toward him with a rumbling that shortly turned into a roar.

Closer. And suddenly a rifle cracked nearby. And another. The great cloud of dust exploded into a hundred parts, reforming swiftly into a huge mass, and seemed to gather more speed the nearer it came. Slocum felt the drumming right up through his horse and saddle.

He waited a moment longer, then dug his heels into the flanks of his horse and it leaped forward to meet the oncoming avalanche of stampeding cattle.

Through the dust Slocum saw the heads and shoulders of the longhorns, two thousand of them, their hooves drilling over the hard ground. Again he heard rifle fire as the desperate beasts drove right at him.

Lifting the spotted pony to a fast canter, he aimed for the center of the stampede, the wiry dust choking him, burning his eyes, cutting his face and hands like a million tiny blades.

The gutsy little horse was well broken and didn't balk at the roaring mass of beef bearing down on them, didn't have to be told to turn quickly when within only a few feet of the leading longhorns; slowing his pace now to keep only a jump ahead of the terrified animals so that Slocum could lean from his saddle and smash at the leaders' muzzles, eyes, and ears with his quirt.

The blows caused the leaders to turn slightly and change their course, though not without the narrowest escape for Slocum and his mount from those razor-pointed horns. In moments they had turned almost completely around and the other cattle followed, forming into a milling, bawling mass.

The swing riders of the herd, who hadn't been able to reach the leaders, pounded up, surrounding the cattle, keeping them milling until as suddenly as it must have started, the stampede was over.

"Run off a few dollars of beef there," Slocum said to a long, stringy man with one blind eye who rode up on a big sorrel stud horse with white stockings.

"You one of LeFort's men?"

The words snapped at him, Slocum catching the hot smell of anger in the other man, the slight move toward the holstered sixgun. Not an overt gesture; small, but clearly a move that would back trouble. Under that wide-brimmed Stetson hat the cattleman's wrinkled face was as tough as leather.

Slocum didn't care a damn. He took his time answering, his green eyes glinting like a lynx as he measured every inch of the lean, angry rider. He said, "You can let go that hard-on, mister, and by God thank me for saving your herd."

The lean man sniffed at that, his body stiffened, and he turned his good eye to the cattle, letting his right hand fall loosely away from the gun butt and onto the pommel of the dusty saddle.

"Should of figgered if you was one of LeFort's men you wouldn't be stoppin' a stampede. I owe you one on my gettin' previous there." He sniffed again. "Name's Otis Dinwiddie. I own this here herd, which I aim to drive to Kansas for shipping. The LeForts got me a touch edgy, stampeding the herd, and 'specially since they shot up my trail foreman."

He spat angrily over his horse's withers, but downwind, and squinted with his good eye toward Slocum, as though seeing him for the first time. "You want a job? I sure like the way you handle that pony and what you done with the herd."

"Eli Case sent me."

The other man's bushy eyebrows shot up and he

pursed his lips. "Eli must of been reading it right along with me, by God." He canted his head toward Slocum as he said, "You got a name?"

"Yep, I do."

Otis Dinwiddie's head turned as two of the swing riders came up. His gaze swung back to the man who had saved his herd, and he waited.

Slocum let him wait a beat. "Slocum," he said finally, and his eyes bored into the bridge of the cattleman's nose.

One of the swing riders let a low whistle escape him, while his employer rubbed his long nose with his thumb knuckle.

"Like I said, Eli knows I need the help. I have heard of you, Slocum. Heard you rode with Quantrill," Dinwiddie said.

"Eli hired me to make sure your herd gets to Abilene, since he's figuring to buy it from you." Slocum had never favored reference to his days with Quantrill and his boys, and his vinegar tone let the other man know it.

Dinwiddie's wrinkled face darkened. "Good enough," he said, and suddenly pressed his hand on his hip, evidently easing pain or age. Then he straightened. "The LeForts been stopping everybody trying to drive north. They're aiming to make the market New Orleans and no other."

"Eli aims to build the market in Kansas," Slocum said.

Suddenly Dinwiddie kicked the big sorrel close to Slocum and the spotted pony. He held out his hand. "Mighty glad to have you. I better inform you the LeForts are a numerous bunch of bastards."

"I know one of them," Slocum said, shaking the proffered hand.

"Then you know 'em all. Porky and Print LeFort have already stampeded this herd six times, and I still ain't acrost the Red River. Jesus!"

Slocum shifted in his saddle, his eyes studying the cattle, scanning the horizon. "They won't stampede 'em after you cross the Red."

"What d'you mean by that?" Otis Dinwiddie's numerous wrinkles tightened into angry surprise.

"That is when they'll start shooting to kill."

One of the swing riders said, "What odds you figger on us gettin' through, then?"

"I'd say ten to one against."

The words froze into the long moment that followed. Some of the riders had come up then and for a while nobody said anything.

"Them's fair odds for a Texan," Dinwiddie said at last. "When do we cross the Red?"

"As soon as possible." Slocum leveled his gaze at the other man. "Tell your men to be ready to start the herd in three hours." And then, remembering, he reached into his shirt pocket and took out the letter. "From Eli Case," he said, handing it to the cattleman.

Dinwiddie took it with a certain hesitation. Slocum could see he didn't like taking orders.

"We made twelve miles with the herd today," the cattleman said. "And they stampeded to boot. They're dead tired, and so are the men. Tomorrow would be better."

"Tired cattle don't stampede so easy," Slocum countered. "We have got to drive them at night, and that's dangerous. You can only do it when they're real tired."

Dinwiddie still didn't like it. Slocum could see it all over him. The drover was an ornery cuss, no question, but he wasn't a fool. He nodded finally.

"Slocum, by God, you like to nub a man up close, I will say."

"I aim to get this herd to Abilene while they still got beef on their carcasses."

Dinwiddie sniffed, then said, "I mind your sayin' you knew one of the LeForts." And he opened his eyes wide, making the shrewd point.

"I appear to have unfinished business with one of those gents," Slocum said, well aware of what the other was driving at. "This here with the herd comes first. 'Course, if the man happens to get himself in front of my sights..." He let it hang, reading the glint in Dinwiddie's good eye as appreciative humor.

And then something that could have been a smile came out of all those wrinkles on the cattleman's sour face as he said, "We'll get Pete to rustle us some grub and coffee then."

3

By the War's end the plains of Texas were dotted with thousands of cattle. During the fighting the longhorns had been left to roam and increase at will, because there were too few men to handle them.

Soldiers, returned from the fighting, established ranches and thought of markets for beef while the greedy eyes of two empires—one new, the other old, rich, and ruthless—looked at this vast wealth on the hoof and fought to control it.

The LeFort brothers had lost their New Orleans cotton empire in the War and now sought to build even bigger with Texas cattle. But the railroad had suddenly come to Kansas, up north, and with it Eli Case, who also had his dream of a kingdom.

There were others with vision in the late Sixties who realized what was happening, knew that destiny was being shaped, and were convinced of their part in it. And bigger names would come later; but at the moment the LeForts and Eli Case were the principal actors in the Texas cattle drama. And, from a different aspect, there was John Slocum.

Slocum clearly saw what was taking place, but he refused to get involved, true to his nature. He had his own journey, and it wasn't along the road to empire. The thousand dollars Case was paying him to get Dinwiddie's KC herd to the market in Abilene was just the ticket. It would be short, maybe not so sweet, but if he lived then there would be other actions, other trails, and the cherished freedom he had always refused to compromise.

"See, Eli, he figgers he can control the whole of the Eastern market." Dinwiddie warmed to his own words as he and Slocum sat by the sparse fire drinking their coffee.

Dinwiddie was telling him pretty much what Eli Case had already said, though his delivery was more colorful: spitting, scratching, probing his crotch, lowering an eyelid to emphasize a point, while his jaws, loose with spittle and tobacco, worked like a prairie dog's, though never missing a word.

"It was the railhead coming put the stop to the brothers; coming to Kansas, I am saying. 'Fore that, they had it all their way and set their own price." Dinwiddie eased his weight, cursing his leg, or hip, rubbing a knuckle deep into his blind eye socket.

"I hear it is two dollars a head," Slocum said, to keep the conversation going, for though he had already heard it all, he had found that often another version could give a fresh and sometimes valuable perspective.

"Down to a dollar now."

"Jesus..."

Dinwiddie wagged his head, pleased at scoring. "Yep. They dropped it after they busted half a dozen herds and about ended any notion of a drive to Kansas."

"Even with Eli offering ten to fifteen, they still aren't bringing up herds, then."

"That is the size of it. The Texans, they are tough boys, but they ain't suicidal and they ain't professional killers; and while Eli is paying ten to fifteen a head, the lead in your guts is thrown in for free." The wink was slow and solemn on the long, wrinkled face. "Last year Bill Buttering tried to push a herd of about five hundred up north. Shit, they made it acrost the Red River and headed for the Cookson Hills." Dinwiddie spat suddenly at the center of the fire. "Everything went just peachy till they come to a pass in the hills. The hull lot of 'em was cut right off at the pockets, by God!"

"I have heard it is good country for ambush," Slocum said drily. And, looking at the cattleman's leathery face, he was sure he could see dust in some of those wrinkles.

"Those boys with Bill had about as much chancet as a fart in a windstorm. Same thing with the Pendergasts, John and Tommy, took a thousand critters. They took gunmen along. Didn't do no good; not a damn bit. There was other herds, but none never got but a few miles the other side of the Red."

"Anyone shipping to New Orleans now?"

"Some are fixin' to."

"But you are pointing your animals north to Kansas."

"That I am; leastways, with you I am." The reply fell hard into the evening that was dropping quietly around them.

"Why?"

Otis Dinwiddie studied it a minute before he could answer. He scratched himself in the armpit, poked at his crotch, and then said, "I am crazy, that is why. Hell, I am a Texian," he went on, using the word in the old way, and he looked at Slocum from the shadow beneath the wide brim of his hat. "Let me tell you, the gather was a true son of a bitch. You know yourself these here brush cows are the orneriest brutes a man can come up against."

"Where did you pick 'em up?"

"Dug 'em out of the canebrakes and blackjacks

along the San Antonio and Guadalupe rivers. Why, some of them beasts hadn't seen a human since being a small calf, and then only when they wuz branded. And we had wild horses to boot. From Mexico! It took two weeks 'fore we even started the gather to get them horses bridle-wise and another two weeks to get 'em so's they'd turn a cow." He paused, wiping spittle from his mouth with the back of his hand.

Slocum said, "Most look to be three to six years, I'd say."

Dinwiddie nodded. "Got a few older; fair amount of she-stuff. Morgan, thank God, knew how to work them; he was a real brush-hopper. We built big corrals with wings a good half-mile from either side of the main gate and then put tame cattle near the mouth of the wings, and then the men would drive the brutes in. The oldest—the real brush-smart buggers—we roped 'em, hog-tied 'em, and left them for a day or so, then necked 'em with a tame animal to drive them into the corral, where they'd stay several days without water or food. Then we'd herd and graze them, then again keep them in the corral a couple of days. And like that again. Jesus!"

The cattleman spat in vigorous appreciation of his difficulties. And Slocum nodded in support, a wry expression on his face. He knew the Texas brush country.

"Those old moss-backs will give a man more trouble than you can shake a stick at, for sure," he said.

Dinwiddie was working his mouth, but not saying anything. Then, "What I am sayin', I ain't giving in to them LeFort sons of bitches. Not when I bin through all that. I figgered me an' Morg could do 'er. Morg was a top drover and real handy with a gun. But, shit, he ain't doin' me a bit of good planted out in boot hill with all that lead holding him down." He spat with sudden venom. "And then—then I need Case's money." He paused. "I ain't as old as I look, Slocum. I am carrying my share of lead. Wife died while I was runnin' the War for General Lee, but I got me a new woman now and we'll settle down once I get the herd through and Case pays me those good prices." He blinked. "Besides, sometimes the only thing for a man to do is what's there needs doing."

Always the dream, Slocum reflected. How often he had heard it. He'd even dreamed it himself: the outfit, the few hundred head of cattle. For him it had been the hope of a horse ranch in the Wind River Mountains. Plenty of good feed there. He'd gotten as far as making overtures to some of the Nez Percés for a bunch of their spotted ponies that they raised on the Pacific slope of the Rockies. Though the deal had fallen through, the dream wasn't finished. It still carried in his night thoughts.

"They got Porky LeFort handling business down around San Antone," Dinwiddie was saying. He picked up a tiny branch and with one end of it began drawing in the dirt. "Like I told you, it's been Porky and Print harassing the herd this while."

"You sure?"

The cattleman glared out of his suddenly darkening face. "You doubtin' my word, mister?"

Suddenly Slocum laughed. "No, I am not doubting you, Mr. Dinwiddie," he said easy, and he liked the older man. He liked it that he'd found himself another woman, he liked his still having guts. By golly, that man had to be sixty-five, maybe more.

"But I have seen Comanche sign on my way north. Not too far from here," Slocum went on.

Dinwiddie's jaw dropped. "No, it was LeFort. You heard those rifles. They was Henrys." He was holding the branch in his two hands now and suddenly he broke it in two. "'Course, the LeForts I know bin using the Indians to keep the herds out. And not just Comanches. Tod Wills told me they run into Kiowa and Arapaho, some of 'em whiskeyed."

"You say the LeForts have been slipping whiskey to the tribes?"

"They have done worse."

"The sign I picked up showed a big party heading west," Slocum said. "The thing is, they could circle back, or there could be others, too."

Dinwiddie's big hat moved as his head bent sagely and he tossed down the two pieces of branch he'd been drawing with.

Slocum picked up one of the pieces and with his other hand wiped the ground smooth. "Porky and the boys will be figuring us to take the Abilene through the Wichita Mountains to Kansas," he said, "it being the only cattle trail through the Indian Territory." He drew a circle in the dirt. "The rest of the LeFort bunch have got to be at about this point here in the Cookson Hills waiting to drygulch us in one of those canyons." He looked closely at the man across the little cookfire. "They'll be waiting to hear from Porky and Print when we cross the Red. I calculate Porky and the boys will be pulling back to Red River Station to wait now, that being where we will have to cross. Soon as we do they'll send word up into the hills to the rest of the gang so they'll be ready."

"Clean as a tooth," muttered Dinwiddie, and he let a sigh run through the whole length of his body.

"It is." Slocum drew a zigzag line in the dust, and

at one of the turns he marked a cross.

"What is that?"

"A trail is where you make it in this country. This cross here is Coyote Ford, forty miles west of Red River Station." Slocum paused, tapping the stick lightly in the dirt. "We're only about fifteen miles from Coyote Ford now."

"So what? We still got to get to Red River Station."

"That is what the LeForts are counting on."

"Shit, man, it's the only place to cross, and the only crossing that meets up with the trail to Abilene."

"That's what I know. And what the LeForts know." He raised his head and looked right at Dinwiddie. "But we are going to cross at Coyote Ford."

"Christ..."

"And we'll head straight north, staying in the Chickasaw country."

"That place is as wild as a whore's drawers on a Saturday night. We got to cut our own trail, for Christ's sake!"

"It will give us time. And time is what we need most."

Dinwiddie pursed his lips, his good eye studying the map in the dust. "I see I shouldn't of told you all that about fighting with the brush cows, by God," he said ruefully.

Slocum grinned at that. "I knew you'd take it right," he said. "Porky and Print will wait at Red River Station a couple of days," he went on. "And when they don't see us it'll take them a couple of days more to find where the herd crossed at Coyote Ford and headed north. Add a day, maybe two, for them to get the news to their brothers in the hills, and we have got a little time."

"But how can you be sure that Porky and Print will

be back at Red River Station?" Dinwiddie wanted to know.

"I am figuring they'll see us just moving the herd along easy, like we're feeling they're leaving us alone for a spell. Remember, they haven't been able to turn you back in six, seven tries. So they'll wait now to get you good."

"Got our guard down, they'll be thinking."

"They will want to hit us on the ground they choose, and they can afford to take their time. The longer they wait, the softer we'll be, is how they'll see it. They could have hit us with the whole bunch back yonder, but they didn't. I read it that they want a sure thing. A real rubout. I've got a feeling they're really wanting to settle something."

"It is chancey, and I hope you're guessin' it correct," Dinwiddie allowed, not a little bit sour.

"Isn't it what you'd do if you was them?"

Dinwiddie didn't answer, but Slocum knew he had scored the point as he went on. "And I will be scouting our back trail as well as point and flanks." He touched the brim of his Stetson with his forefinger, pushing it back on his head. "It'll be dark soon. Better get the men to rest." He took off his hat and resettled it on his head. "I'll be taking a look about." He stood up.

Dinwiddie pushed himself to his feet and stomped his game leg to get the circulation going. Squinting at his new trail boss, he said, "I know they want to settle it once for all." He paused, working his jaws as though getting ready to say something more, or maybe just to spit.

"A while back when I was the law in Toro Wells, down in Llano County, there was the Hogan gang." Now he did spit. "One day they rode in aiming to tree the town." With a grunt, he shifted his weight. "That's when I got this, and this." He indicated his eye and his leg. "And this..." He held up his right hand, flexing the fingers stiffly.

"What happened?"

"The boys, they are still in Toro Wells, the three of them." He paused to spit again and, suddenly coughing, almost lost his chew. "One got away, however, carrying lead, and he vowed he would come back. He never."

Slocum wondered why Dinwiddie was telling him the story, but though he had already seen how the cattleman liked to talk, he realized that his stories had a point.

"He never come back," Dinwiddie resumed. "The son of a bitch died in bed. His sons said on account of the package of blue whistlers from the goose gun which about cut him plumb in two."

"And his name was LeFort?"

Otis Dinwiddie was regarding the horizon, and he spoke now as though reading the words on those distant hills. "His boys called him Daddy. Famous he was, and his boys. Daddy LeFort. But this time he'd ridden with his cousin Jake Hogan: probably a favor or payback of some kind."

"The boys know for sure it was yourself, do they?"

The cattleman nodded. "You said they're looking to settle something. It isn't only the herd, is what I am saying. Things get personal like that, it can get real ropey." He reached to the pocket of his hickory shirt and brought out his plug of chewing tobacco. "I do wonder sometimes if those boys ever had a mother. I never heard tell of one." And he winked solemnly at Slocum, bringing out his big skinning knife to slice off a chew.

"Well, Dinwiddie, it can be just that personal business that can throw them. They can get anxious. Anyhow, we'll be two against the seven instead of just the one."

"Make that six."

Slocum cocked his head. "I thought there were seven brothers."

"Goose LeFort, he is still in the penitentiary. Folsom, I do believe." A strange grin began to seep into the lined face as Slocum watched. "But I also believe those six boys'll do their very best to make up for brother Goose's absence."

At eleven o'clock that night the pickets roused the sleeping men. Cursing into the clear, moonlit night, they pulled on boots, checked their weapons, saddled and mounted their horses, and began working the cattle into two long lines. Soon the two thousand longhorns stretched in a double line over half a mile long. The point men rode at the head of the herd, while the swing riders were placed by Slocum at intervals on each side, keeping the cattle in formation and nudging them along with the ends of their lariat ropes used as whips, though some of the men had quirts.

At the rear of the herd were the dragmen, their bandannas pulled up over their faces, hats jammed low on their heads, eyes slitted against the insistent wall of gritty dust raised by the trailing cattle. Some had blankets thrown over their heads, which still didn't give full protection against the dust.

Next came the remuda, the fresh horses with the two wranglers. At the very end of the line rode the chuck wagon pulled by four mules with Heavy Pete, the cook, and the camp supplies: corn meal, sorghum molasses, beans, salt, sugar, coffee; and branding irons, some axes and shovels, horse-shoeing tools and fresh horseshoes, and extra guns and ammunition, plus the men's bedding.

Slocum rode up and down the line, cautioning the men to keep quiet, other than the low singing some of them engaged in to calm the cattle. For the most part, he felt Dinwiddie and his late trail boss had picked a fair crew. They were the usual trail-toughened hands, wearing their hats as part of their anatomy, speaking real salty, defining their occupation through stringent humor and frequent reference to the deity.

But Slocum had been around too long to allow that everything was as smooth as it appeared. He knew there had to be something Dinwiddie and his trail boss had missed, human nature being what it was, plus the LeForts being what they were. Along about two hours later he found it.

He had just checked the point men, reminding them that they were close to Comanche country and, while the tribes were keeping the peace, it was not to be taken for granted. Meat was scarce for the Indians, and all that beef on the hoof would surely be tempting.

He was riding a chunky little strawberry roan taken from the remuda while his own horse rested. The roan was full of fun when Slocum stepped into the saddle, and had started to crowhop, trying to buck, but Slocum, pulling tight on the reins, wouldn't let him get his head down. But the roan was a tough cow pony, he was glad to see, as he rode back down the line of trudging cattle.

Suddenly his eye caught the flame of a lucifer and he kneed the roan over to two riders who were sitting their horses by a low cutbank.

"Put that light out, God damn it! You heard the orders!"

"Who the hell are you?" came the voice. "You

don't sound like Dinwiddie, by God!" The words rasped out, carrying with them the smell of whiskey.

Slocum brought the roan right up against the rider who had spoken. "The name is Slocum, mister, and you remember that!" The back of his hand hard across the other man's face almost knocked him out of his saddle. And as the other's hand streaked to his holster, Slocum grabbed him by the collar and pulled him right off his horse, dumping him on the ground. He heard the small shattering of glass as the bottle landed on something hard.

Slocum was not finished. His hand swept to his own sixgun and brought the steel barrel down on the second man's wrist as he started to draw.

The cry of pain was charged with fury, and Slocum saw the man on the ground pulling at his holster.

"Hold it—or you're both taking up permanent residence!"

Both froze at the click of the hammer on Slocum's Colt as it was drawn back.

"There'll be no drinking on this drive unless I order it. And, by God, then you *will* drink! You make one more funny move, either one of you, and I'll peel the skin off the both of you and leave you for buzzard bait. You understand me?"

The man on the horse nodded, and his companion on the ground mumbled something which Slocum chose to take as agreement.

"You are riding swing, but you stay on opposite sides of the herd. I don't want to see you two together again till we get to Abilene." He pointed the Colt toward the man on the ground. "Get on your horse."

They sat their horses, watching him in silence.

"Get moving," he told them. "And remember one thing: I am ahead of you boys. No matter what you're figuring, I've already figured it first."

"Slocum, we wasn't doing anything..." the one nearest him started to say.

"Keep it like that, then."

As they turned their horses the other man said, "God damn it, you like to broke my wrist!"

"Use your other one."

When they had ridden off he felt a strange sense of relief that the action had taken place, that something that he had suspected beneath the surface had come to a boil and shown itself.

Listening to Slocum's report later that night, Otis Dinwiddie's wrinkles seemed to increase. "Dutch Dillman and Box Wagner." The cattleman's bony jaws raced over the names in his anger. "They are a couple of kids, sixteen like, fancy theirselves with the guns. You know I had a notion, but Morg, he talked me into it. Said we had to have hands who could handle iron, not just push cows. Well, we took 'em on. Far as cow work neither one's worth a pocket of cold piss. But, shit, we do need firepower. Just be careful. You've got a reputation, and those two young buggers could want to build on it."

Slocum scratched the side of his jaw.

"What I am saying, a man can get shot just as dead from the back as he can from the front," Dinwiddie went on.

"I will watch both. I never did like the idea of being shot either way."

"You want to get rid of 'em?"

"Not yet. We let them loose they'll maybe trail us and try to even it when we're taken with something else, or they could maybe join up with Porky and Print." And then he added, "Unless they're working for them already."

Dinwiddie's heavy eyebrows rose into his forehead. Then he lowered an eyelid and raised it slowly, his dead eyeball appearing like a marble in the white burst of moonlight. "You know, Slocum, I about figured likewise."

Slocum nodded, turning the roan toward the drag. "Me too," he said.

And Otis Dinwiddie, long on experience, didn't spoil the humor of the exchange by allowing his own smile to reach further than his eyes.

In the tender light of pre-dawn the longhorns and drovers slipped into view, appearing on the land neither swiftly nor hesitantly, yet all at once they were quite there, solidly defined under the sharp pewter sky, with the land crackling now as it heated up.

When they reached the creek Slocum ordered a halt to make camp. He set the pickets and when breakfast was done, they were relieved and came in to eat Heavy Pete O'Hay's flapjacks washed down with Arbuckle coffee. As the sun rose, burning away the overcast, some of the men broke out a deck of cards and a desultory game of stud started up. Others spread their bedrolls and turned in.

"Could be fixin' to storm some, I'd say." Heavy Pete O'Hay studied the horizon as he leaned against a wheel of the chuck wagon and regarded the new trail boss. Legend maintained that there had been a time when Heavy Pete had been thin as a finger, but had one day entered a pie-eating contest in Junction City, and had won. Since that time he'd traveled the country entering pie-eating contests and invariably winning. His weight and size had changed accordingly. But Heavy had made the mistake of entering a contest to see how many pies he could bite through at the same time, the pies being stacked one on top of the other. Some bettor, eager to insure his winnings at Heavy's expense, had slipped a pie tin into the stack, with the result that Heavy Pete had broken out nearly all his front teeth. Yet, though he immediately stopped entering pie contests, and even eating pies, Pete never returned to his former size and weight. And in some quarters he was still known as the pie-eating champion of the Pecos and points west.

"Got some coffee, have you?" Slocum asked.

Heavy Pete pointed, then followed the direction of his rusty-looking finger with a firm jet of brown saliva.

Slocum was relieved to see that this fell short of the coffee pot. He picked up a tin cup, wiped it clean with his fingers, and poured.

"You figger we'll make it, huh?" Heavy Pete cleared his throat loudly.

"That is what we are aiming at."

"You don't mind the LeFort boys."

"I mind them, but we are heading for Kansas, and that is the size of it."

Heavy Pete's thick whiskers suddenly stirred as he evidently pursed his lips, which were all but invisible under all that hair. His eyes grew as round as silver dollars.

"I am with you there, trail boss. I am only sayin' it ain't going to be easy."

"That's what I know."

"I hear you braced them two—Wagner and Dillman."

"Had an exchange of words." He sipped carefully at the steaming coffee.

"Watch your back with them two is what I am saying." Heavy Pete nodded to emphasize the importance of his words. "I see they been drinking the whiskey."

"Not any more."

The camp cook regarded him from beneath lowered lids for a moment, his big hands on his big hips, his big belly hanging over his big wide belt. "And Gans LeFort," he said softly, his eyes still on Slocum, the hairs in his big nose flickering as he breathed heavily. "Jesus, might be we will by God make it to Kansas!"

"Excepting first we got to get across the Red River," Slocum said.

4

Around the middle of the afternoon one of the point men came pounding in to where Slocum was riding alongside Dinwiddie, with the cattle strung over an open area between two creeks.

"I'd say a dozen braves up ahead. Comanche, I do believe, and pretty gussied up. Looks like they'll be visiting."

The rider was a stubby man with a big jaw which he shoved forward now as he finished his message.

"They looking for a fight?" Slocum asked.

"More like hunters, I'd say. They got a couple of old flintlocks, some bows and arrers, coup sticks, too."

Slocum jerked his thumb. "Get back on point. We'll bunch the herd. Tell the men as you go." He turned to Dinwiddie as the rider galloped away on a big hammerhead bay. "I'll check the left flank, you take the right. Let 'em come on in easy."

"The drag?"

"They ain't going anywhere but where we'll be when we've got the cows bunched. Send a man back to tell them, anyway."

Shortly, Slocum rode up a draw and from a stand of box elders counted thirteen young warriors as they rode slowly toward the clearing where Dinwiddie and his men were bunching the herd. Carefully he noted the flintlocks, the bows and arrows, the lances, knives, and tomahawks, and the coup sticks. Fairly well armed, he decided, but not equal to the KC's firepower.

When he rode back the cattle were still milling about, but calmer now as the drovers pushed them closer together. By the time the Indian party broke across the creek and started walking their horses toward the cattlemen, Slocum had stationed the drovers the way he wanted them.

Slocum spoke some fair Sioux, pretty good Piegan, and he was a good talker of sign, which was the common language of the plains, so he didn't hesitate to take the initiative.

"Greetings," he signed as three Indians detached themselves from the main body of visitors and rode forward, while the others moved out in a small semicircle and waited. "Are you hunting? We saw buffalo tracks one sleep ago."

The three Indians wore breechclouts and leggins, and their bodies were painted. The one in the middle wore a single feather in his scalp lock; his companions wore only headbands.

"You are on our land," the middle Indian said, signing. "You pay chuck-away."

His companions grunted and looked at the nearest longhorns.

"We offer tobacco," Slocum said, showing the sack he had already prepared.

The Indian who had signed was young, with a scar along his right jaw. He accepted the tobacco, scowling. Slocum was watching as many of the party as he could. They were all young, alert on their ponies, their faces showing no expression whatsoever.

"You suspicioning them, too," Dinwiddie said at his side.

"First place, this ain't their land," Slocum said. "They're not Comanches, that is sure."

"You going to tell them?"

The Indian with the single feather was signing, "You pay chuck-away."

"We will not pay chuck-away. We have offered tobacco because we wish to keep peace with you; but this is not your land. This is Comanche land. You are not Comanche."

The Indian who had done all the signing held up two fingers. "Pay two chuck-away."

"No," Slocum signed quickly, and then added, as his right hand dropped to his holster, "We are friends. We are passing through here."

There followed a long pause while the three Indians conferred. Then, raising himself on his brown and white pony, his dark eyes piercing Slocum, the Indian with the single feather spat over his horse's withers and signed that he and his warriors were men and had no use for dogs. The other two Indians immediately followed suit, spitting and signing that the white men were dogs.

The exchange had taken a while, and Slocum could feel the restlessness of the cattlemen.

"Save it for the LeForts, boys," he called over his shoulder. Signing to the Indian now, he said, "You come from LeFort? What are you doing this far away from Arapaho country? This is Comanche country. The Comanches are many and strong. They will wipe you out."

"We and Comanche are friends. I am Little Coyote. You pay chuck-away!"

"Where is your chief?" Slocum signed. "You are not a chief."

The Indian did not answer. Instead, he and his companions spat again, scowling and muttering, and, turning their ponies angrily, making obscene gestures with their fingers, they cantered back to their waiting party. Minutes later they were gone back down the trail from where they had come.

"They could be trouble," Dinwiddie said. "Did you smell the whiskey on them?"

"I also spotted a pretty new-looking rifle barrel sticking out from a blanket on one of them in the back. I'd say they had more firepower than they were showing."

"Think they're working with the LeForts?"

"Somebody got them that whiskey, and somebody got them that rifle." He looked toward the creek where the Indians had crossed. "I'd say the LeForts aren't taking any chances. They've likely got this whole country scouted with friendlies from the Comanches and Kiowa as well as Araps." He ran his big hand along the side of his jaw. "I'd say we don't have as much of that extra time as we'd thought, Mr. Dinwiddie."

"But what the hell they're doing this far down from their own country is what I want to know."

"Like I say, they could be hired by the LeForts. They could also be a bunch of young bucks run off for some excitement. Hell, it's spring, ain't it?"

By nightfall they had reached the Red River with no further sign of the Arapahoes. They were still a short distance from Coyote Ford. Slocum ordered camp in a strong position on a sharp bend where the banks were steep and the waters deep, so that in case of an attack the Indians could not approach from the river side.

He was expecting trouble. And it hit. But it wasn't the Indians.

The storm came just at the edge of night, showing dark over the low range of hills on the horizon, then sweeping down fast with the opening gusts of wind that rode in toward the bedded herd like an advance party, bending trees and grass, tossing the manes and tails of the horses, spooking the cattle who bellowed to their feet, rolling their eyes, pawing the ground in fear. In the strange, silvery light the men raced to their horses.

A drop of rain fell. Then another. And in a moment there came a patter and suddenly a great drumbeat of water bulleting down. The sky was totally black, and now forked with stark lightning that turned the world to day, followed by a blinding crack of thunder with the riders pressing close to the cattle, hunched under their rain gear, but soaking wet all the same as their mounts sloshed around the terrified beasts.

"Shit take it!" Dinwiddie shouted. "If it ain't the damn Injuns it's the weather!"

"And if it ain't the weather it's the Indians," Slocum shot back as he snapped the leather-sewn end of his lariat rope at a longhorn that looked as though he was going to charge head-on at the spotted pony and rider.

Again lightning split the entire sky, the thunder sounding as though it would break the earth into pieces. Slocum watched the lightning playing on the great horns of the cattle.

Suddenly a tremendous bolt struck nearby. It seemed to Slocum that half of the milling, terrified cattle were knocked down. It stunned him, and for a moment he wondered if he had gone deaf as his horse fell to the ground. The animal was up in an instant, but Slocum was left lying on the ground, still gripping the reins, unable to move. With a terrified snort the pony attempted to run, but Slocum held him. Another flash tore the sky, lighting the maddened cattle in brilliant outlines. Slocum felt a great thump on the back of his head.

When he came to his senses he was in a sitting position and across his knees lay the neck of a dead Texas steer. With the next flash of lightning he could see dead longhorns lying all around him, while the din of hundreds of cattle knocking their horns together and bellowing as they stampeded seemed to be passing right over him.

He realized then what had happened as he threw himself as close to the body of the dead steer as possible, so close that his head was between its front legs while he curled up as tightly as he could.

The longhorns were running and jumping in every direction. Suddenly he remembered what he had heard before, that a stampeding herd would never run over a man or animal lying on the ground. He prayed that the cattle knew it, too, as he tried to make himself even smaller.

Finally the racing beasts were past, but he could see nothing in the complete darkness. And when he called out there was no answer. Wherever he was, he was alone in the pelting rain. His horse was gone, and there was nothing he could do but wait until the sky lightened and he could see.

Shortly before dawn the rain stopped, and when the first gray light began to steal over the land, Slocum stood up. He discovered that he was at the bottom of a small hill; he began to move slowly, feeling himself for breaks and cuts. There were no animals to be seen, nor any humans. He was still alone. His foot hurt, but he saw no blood, and supposed he had simply twisted it.

Feeling stiff and sore all over, he began to climb to the top of the hill. He discovered that not a hundred yards to the north the chuck wagon was standing undamaged. His foot was hurting him more as he hobbled toward it. To his astonishment, there stood his little spotted pony, waiting meek as a lamb, as though nothing at all had happened.

The wagon was deserted, but there was some cold food, which he ate quickly as he boiled black coffee. Then he examined his foot more closely, discovering that his spur had been wrenched from his right boot and his heel was burned. Pretty close. And he felt something vibrate through him as he realized just how close it had been. Rarely had he considered how his life might end; he had never thought it might be from a bolt of lightning.

Mounting the pony, he headed northeast, in the direction most of the stampeded herd seemed to have taken. As he rode through the deep mud along the river bottom, he wondered how he and the spotted pony had survived. The land where the cattle had run away looked ravaged.

Topping the next hill he came to, he saw Heavy Pete O'Hay riding one of the chuck wagon mules bareback with the remuda horses.

"Me an' Burt held 'em, by God," the big man exclaimed the moment he saw Slocum. "I wouldn't of believed it but by God we did!"

"Where's Burt now?" Slocum asked. He was astonished to see the remuda together.

"We lost two, the little dun and the buckskin," Heavy Pete said. "Burt went lookin'." The cook was pale; he was sweating. His eyes were wider than usual, Slocum realized, strangely staring. "By God," Pete said, "I could stand something stronger to drink than water or Arbuckle coffee, let me tell you!"

"Well, see if you can dig up something," Slocum said. "We all of us need it. The wagon's yonder. I'll see who I can find and we can gather back there."

In a few moments he had roped a fresh horse out of the remuda. It took him the better part of the morning to locate all the men. Dinwiddie had been kicked in his game leg and was cursing a streak when Slocum found him hobbling near a narrow ravine that had been washed out in the hillside.

Gradually the men collected. Some had suffered injuries, but none serious. The cattle were spread all over the country.

"Gone to hell and breakfast," Dinwiddie said when the crew was finally together and having coffee and some grub at the chuck wagon.

Some of them had come in with cattle, and now Slocum ordered the crew to start a wide swing and bring in anything they came across, KC or otherwise.

"Slocum, for Christ's sake, how about a rest! You want to kill us off?" Dutch Dillman was holding up his pistol-whipped arm, which was wrapped in a torn blue bandanna.

"Not unless necessary," Slocum replied, the words coming out hard.

"He likes to fun!" Box Wagner's thin wet face was twisted red with anger as he spoke from beside his companion. "Likes to remind us he's big John Slocum what rode with Quantrill!"

Slocum was tired. He was tired of young punks trying to hooraw him for a reputation. But he didn't waste a beat. "Get your asses into them saddles. I mean right now!" His hand moved to within a couple of inches of the holstered .31. "We are going to get that herd together. You want to settle something with me, you two? We'll handle that right now, or it can wait." He paused about the space of a breath. "You decide! I mean right now!"

He was sitting his horse tight but easy, his right hand loose and ready, his eyes quick as light.

They let him have the round, their mouths, eyes, lean young bodies snapping with hatred as they mounted their horses.

"You're the boss, Mr. Slocum," Wagner said with soft menace. And the two of them kicked their weary horses into a gallop.

Late that afternoon Slocum ordered a count. The herd was strung out in a long, uneven line, and two men rode ahead some distance, taking up positions on either side of the head cattle. The pointers now squeezed the longhorns in, narrowing the string that passed between the two counters. When a hundred cattle had been counted, without taking his eyes from the cattle the counter tied a knot in his saddle string. When the counting was all done the knots showed that they were short seventy head, not including the carcasses of twenty steers killed by the lightning.

That night Slocum had the cattle bedded out on the prairie far from any timber or streams. During the night the jittery animals made a number of attempts to stampede, but each time they were thrown back.

And it was over. An orchestra of birds brought the wet-smelling dawn, revealing the land in a dazzling conjunction of water and steam as the sun rose above the horizon, while on the branches of the trees and on the blades of grass, too, drops of water danced light in every direction, and the freshly minted sky held the world.

With the taste of sour coffee in their mouths, Slocum and half a dozen men rode out to check the herd. The cattle were intact, but the horse herd had vanished, and young Burt Kagan the wrangler had taken an arrow in the fleshy part of his arm, while a blow on the back of his head had knocked him completely out.

"The Comanche?" a man asked.

"Araps," Slocum said, tapping the green markings on the arrow.

All the horses except the seven they were riding were missing.

"It could be they're aiming to split us," Slocum said to Dinwiddie as he picked four men to accompany him.

"If they hit here we'll handle 'em," the cattleman promised.

"Get those breastworks up," said Slocum. "I'll leave you three horses. Keep 'em well hidden. They'll be looking for them." He tightened the cinch on the spotted pony. "They have left piss-poor sign."

"You can thank the storm," Dinwiddie said. "You'll be guessing more than some."

Slocum stepped into the stirrup. "We can maybe count on one thing."

"What's that?" The cattleman squinted up at the man on the horse.

"Most of those braves were real young. They'll be puffed up, singing their brag. It could make them careless."

"You want the Sharps?" Dinwiddie asked, referring to the buffalo gun he had in the chuck wagon.

"You'll need it. If they've got Henrys they'll use 'em here." He nodded in the direction of Dillman and Wagner. "You want me to take them two?"

Dinwiddie shook his head. "I will wrangle the buggers."

Slocum and the four men rode east. The storm had done severe damage. There were no tracks at all, and he was guessing they would head north, on the assumption that it was the same band of Arapahoes and that they were working for LeFort. Going north would keep them ahead of the herd for another strike.

Not until late in the forenoon did he spot fresh sign of the Indians and the KC remuda. A large number of horses were heading northeast toward comparatively level country, and many of them were shod. They weren't traveling fast. He was right about their being careless.

Slocum led the small, determined party at an easy pace for the next few miles, wanting the horses to be well rested for the encounter. Finally they came to a ridge from the summit of which they could see some Indians driving horses about a mile and a half away.

"There they are," one of the men said.

"We'll move in slow," Slocum cautioned, and turned his pony toward a draw to their right that led in the direction of the horse thieves.

When they were just below the lip of the draw he dismounted. Telling the men to stay where they were, he crept to the brow of the hill. He was in time to see the Arapahoes going over a hill just beyond. Watching until they had disappeared behind the hill, he signaled his men, and together they hurried to the next ridge.

From this ridge they could plainly see the Indians, counting four. That left nine to attack Dinwiddie and the herd, figuring they were the same band that had demanded payment.

The four Arapahoes ahead had just halted to change horses.

"We're in luck," Slocum said. "They're riding their own horses."

Suddenly the Indians caught sight of the KC men, and a shout went up.

Slocum booted the spotted horse into a fast gallop and his men followed right after as the group ahead of them mounted frantically. Whipping their ponies and yelling at the stolen remuda, the Arapahoes tried to make it to a line of timber at the end of a long coulee.

The Indians, riding their grass-fed ponies, were soon overtaken by Slocum's party on bigger horses that had been fed on grain and were swifter and had more staying power. The four Indians were also hampered with the stolen remuda. Getting rattled, they separated—and that was exactly what Slocum wanted.

Their bows and arrows had no chance against the Colts and Henrys of the drovers. Slocum had told his men to pick their targets beforehand, and it paid off. In about five minutes there were two wounded Arapahoes. Their companions had picked them up and raced away, leaving the stolen horses. Not a single KC man had been touched, though a horse had an ear split with an arrow.

Slocum left three men to bring the remuda back while he and a young man named Denny roped and saddled fresh horses and galloped ahead.

They pushed their mounts hard, and it wasn't long before they heard rifle fire. Racing to the crest of a long, low coulee Slocum saw two of the Arapahoes firing Henrys. The others had their flintlocks and bows and arrows. But suddenly the sharp, heavy crack of Dinwiddie's Sharps entered the fray, and Slocum witnessed the accuracy with which the aging man used it. So did the Arapahoes. When Slocum and young

Denny cut in with crossfire from the northeast, they decided they'd had enough.

None of the cowboys had been seriously hit. The Arapahoes had suffered two or three wounded, all of whom were swept onto the horses of the other warriors.

"Dillman and Wagner still with you?" Slocum asked when he dismounted.

The cattleman coughed out an abrupt laugh. "I kept my good eye on the both of them."

"Keep your blind one on them, too," Slocum said. "I got a notion we're going to need it."

"You know, sometimes I think that's right." Dinwiddie nodded in agreement. "There have been times when I know I can about see with the blind one!" He opened his eyes wide, and stuck his tongue deep into his cheek, pushing it out like a ball as he innocently regarded Slocum.

"That is what I am saying, old timer. Looking is one thing, but seeing is something else." And Slocum grinned at the cattleman's instantly sour look.

Around the middle of the afternoon they reached Coyote Ford. Slocum ordered the herd pushed across the Red River. At dusk they threw the cattle on the bed ground. Slocum doubled the night guard.

The next morning he discovered that Dillman and Wagner were gone.

5

Now the light of the spring morning touched the dark plain, feeling its way across the gentle grass which showed no sign of man's passage: no tracks of horses or cows or wagon wheels, but the honest print of buffalo, elk, antelope, and other creatures.

As the light quickened a thrush called in the glistening air, and a band of colors sang over the softening land, awakening the new day. Like a breath the light wind stirred the flowers, the grasses, the rustling leaves. At the creek crossing there were quivering shadows, and the soft, round sound of water in the rocky streambed.

Slocum had shot the buck deer just at dawn, butchered it, and was now packing it back to camp on the little dun packhorse. Topping a rise, he watched a band of geese swinging down the sky. Then he saw the team and wagon.

It was stopped in the clearing below, near a thin creek lined with box elders. From under the canvas sides two rifle barrels were pointed at the four Indians who were walking their horses slowly forward, each of them holding up his right hand in the sign of peace.

Quickly, Slocum dropped from his saddle, and pulled both horses behind a grouping of rocks. He had shot the deer with Dinwiddie's Sharps, and now he drew it easily from its scabbard and found a place in the rocks from where he could sight the Indians who had now stopped at the side of the Conestoga wagon.

He was too far away to hear anything that was said, but he could see one of the riders gesticulating in sign language. He recognized one of them from the Arapaho band, but their leader, with the scar on his jaw, was not present.

Yet whoever was inside the wagon remained hidden, apparently satisfied to let their guns do the talking. Slocum had quickly noted that the Indians carried only bows and arrows and one lance.

He was wondering what a single wagon could be doing this far from a major trail. Some sodbuster and family who'd likely gotten lost, perhaps in the storm, he reasoned.

The Indian spokesman was still gesticulating, and now he raised his voice, but Slocum could not distinguish what was said.

He was more certain now that the Arapahoes were not attached to a large war party but were a renegade band who, like so many young bucks in the springtime, felt the itch to hunt, to war a little, to prove themselves men and warriors, revelling against the constraints of the new and unaccustomed blanket-Indian life so many of their elders had accepted. He couldn't blame them. He knew that if he was a member of one of the tribes, he too would hit the trail.

Suddenly he noticed that one of the Indians was sitting his horse badly, and it crossed his mind that there was whiskey about.

At the same time, he was concerned that the people inside the wagon might get rattled and begin shooting, which could trigger real trouble; trouble that could spread beyond this little confrontation. With the KC herd on his hands, it was no time for an Indian uprising.

Slocum raised the big Sharps and, aiming not too high, pulled the trigger. It was a scare shot. The heavy gun boomed out and the startled Arapahoes spun their horses almost in unison and raced separately out and away from any line of fire from the wagon. Sweeping around the sides, they whipped their ponies toward the far edges of the little creek. Slocum fired a second shot for good measure.

He didn't waste time now, quickly slipping the Sharps back into its scabbard, mounting his horse, and cantering both animals down to the wagon. He was glad to see that the rifle barrels were withdrawn.

By the time he was down on the flat land a man and a woman had climbed out of the wagon and were standing next to the bay team who were cropping the bunch grass, kicking and shaking their heads at flies. Slocum noticed a black saddle horse tied to the other side of the wagon now as he drew rein in front of the man and woman, each of whom was carrying a rifle.

The man was elderly, his face red and lined under a shock of white hair. He was wearing a black broadcloth coat and matching trousers. Even from far away Slocum had noticed that the woman was younger; simply from the way she moved, her air was the air of youth. Even so, he was surprised when he saw her close up. She couldn't have been more than twenty, twenty-two or -three.

As Slocum swung down from his horse, the man spoke.

"We offer thanks to the Lord that you arrived at this most propitious moment, good sir. We were close to the end of our tether, although we did not doubt the true outcome. I take it, sir, that it was you firing at those redskins."

"That's right," Slocum's eyes swept to the girl. "You all right?"

"Thank you. Now—yes." She smiled a gentle smile at him, relief showing clearly.

He was at once taken by her soft, wide-spaced gray eyes, full wide mouth, and brown hair sweeping to the top of her head, where it was tied with a yellow ribbon. She was wearing a loose gingham dress which Slocum decided set off her figure a good deal more provocatively than anything tight-fitting would have done, and he found himself staring at her as the old man cut in.

"My dear..." He placed his hand gently on her arm. "Let us introduce ourselves to our savior here." His smile was quick, professionally genuine, Slocum noted. "I am the Reverend Miller Muldoon, and this is my niece Ava."

"I'm John Slocum, driving a herd of longhorns up to the Kansas market."

The Reverend Muldoon bent his head, his hands together in front of his wide chest. "Ava and myself have been traveling west in search of a community that would benefit from the Lord's teaching. Not..." He held up his hand quickly. "...Not that any and all wouldn't assuredly reap profit from the word of Our Lord, but some are more...shall I say, ready. It has not been an easy task," he continued, his face, neck, shoulders, and entire upper body bending in sanctimonious confidence. "Not an easy task at all!" He had a ringing voice with a slight huskiness to it. "Unfortunately, most unfortunately, the wagon train we signed up with turned out to be filled with the coarsest elements you can imagine. Gamblers, questionable women, and all the rest. Drinkers! You can realize it was no place for my niece. We therefore decided, for our own peace of mind, not to mention physical safety—excuse me, my dear—that it would be better if we left the train." He paused, his eyes washing over Slocum, who had taken out a quirly and was lighting it.

"It goes without saying that we were naive," the Reverend continued. "*I* was naive. I accept full blame for taking us from the frying pan to the fire." His eyes fell fondly on his niece. "My dear..." He turned back to Slocum, who noticed that he had one eye larger than the other; the larger also seemed more penetrating than its companion. "I was so concerned for Ava's safety. Those men...brutes! And then, on top of it all, we got lost in that terrible storm!"

"Uncle, it's all right." She smiled apologetically at Slocum. "It's over now."

Slocum well knew how some of the elements on wagon trains could be. "I'm afraid, Reverend Muldoon, that you're in a more difficult place than the fire or the frying pan you mention," he said. "I believe those Indians were drinking whiskey, and it's only by..."

"...by the grace of God, sir," the Reverend cut in swiftly. "Excuse my interrupting you."

"...that you're both alive," Slocum went on. "It's a good thing you didn't start shooting."

"Why so, sir? They were threatening us; at least, so we believed."

"You could have touched off more than just a shooting. It could have gotten into something bigger. It could have spread. But it's done now, and we can be thankful." Slocum, seeing that the Reverend Muldoon had an argumentative streak in him, swept his words quickly out of the way and turned to the girl.

There was the trace of a smile at the corners of her mouth. "We couldn't have fired our guns if we'd wanted to," she said. "We don't have any ammunition."

Slocum stared at her in amazement. "Jesus Christ..."

The Reverend was already holding up his hands, his bowed head suffering the blasphemy. "Sir, sir, please do not take the Lord's name in such a manner."

"Sorry, Reverend, but, holy... I mean... well, let's forget about it." He caught the laughter creeping into the girl's eyes. "In any case, you can't stay here," he said.

"Will they be back?" Her eyes were wide now, and there was no laughter in them.

The Reverend Muldoon was looking severely at the problem, his eyes on Slocum, his lips pursed. He must have been sixty-some, Slocum decided, though not Dinwiddie's kind of sixty.

"What do you advise us to do, Mr. Slocum?"

"The only thing is to come with me. We'll head back to the drive and then see what we can do. But you can't stay out here alone." He had started to turn toward his horses, but stopped and swung back to the Muldoons. "What did they want from you? Did you understand anything of what they were saying?"

"They wanted whiskey," Reverend Muldoon said. "The devil's brew!"

"They spoke a few words of English," the girl said. "They kept saying 'the whiskey... bring whiskey.' Something like that. It was very strange."

"Did they mention the name LeFort?"

"LeFort? No. No." The Reverend turned to his niece, who shook her head.

"Shit," muttered Slocum, not wholly under his breath.

"Sir?" Reverend Muldoon's raised eyebrows regarded him questioningly and with disapproval. They were large eyebrows over large, yellowish orbs in which were many red lines. His cheeks were red, and he had large, pale ears out of which much hair sprang, as it did from his bulbous, pitted nose.

"Would you like something in the way of tea or coffee, or possibly something to eat, Mr. Slocum?" the girl offered.

"I think we'd better get out of here right now," Slocum declared. "I mean right quick."

"You wish us to accompany you, sir?" The Reverend drew himself to his full height, which physically alone was considerable, and in combination with his astonishing dignity, was a formidable height indeed. But it didn't bother Slocum.

"You're going to have to, Reverend." He turned to Ava Muldoon. "Who'll skin that team?"

"I don't understand."

"Who will drive the horses?"

She smiled. She had very even, white teeth, and he felt that in a way she was almost making fun of his seriousness, and he liked it.

"I drive," she said. And she added, "I am ready."

And Slocum liked that, too.

In the cabin high in the box canyon in the Cookson Hills, the boys were in brisk spirits as they waited for brother Gans to return from Red River Station. Porky and Print had only just arrived that morning, and Gans was expected hourly.

On the rickety wooden table stood a well-punished bottle of whiskey, and under its influence the talk flowed easily, laced with laughter and the constant threat of violence. On such occasions the brothers were as wont to fight with one another as with anyone else.

In the next room, two women were preparing the evening meal. They, too, were enjoying themselves, and had been for some time as the sole recipients of the masculine favors offered so assiduously by the family members in the adjoining room. The only outsider present, in fact, was Dutch Dillman, who had arrived only a while ago with the news that the KC herd had crossed the Red River at Coyote Ford and that John Slocum was ramrodding it. His partner, Box Wagner, had headed directly to Red River Station with the same tidings, though missing Porky and Print and very likely Gans.

"It'll be jackpot poker, gents, jacks or better," Porky announced as he began shuffling the limp, greasy deck of cards which hardly had enough snap to make a sound as he shuffled.

Porky, a man with beetle brow and a big head set on shoulders that had reminded many an adversary of a buffalo, turned his malevolent gaze on the sole nonmember of the LeFort clan. "Dillman, set. I reckon your money's about as good as anybody else's." His words were not warm, and they brought a flush of resentment to Dutch Dillman's wary, tight little face and laughter to Ollie, Print, Ike, and Finn LeFort.

Dutch was a skinny young man who wore a perpetual sneer on his face. He feared the LeForts—there were so many of them—but he had not been afraid of Porky in San Antonio when he'd been offered the job as a spy in the KC crew, along with his pal Box Wagner. One LeFort he was confident of handling; maybe even two. But five or six of them was something else. Dutch was not alone. Others had the same problem. Clearly, six vicious killers were more dangerous—more inevitable—than one. Dutch was cautioning himself to be very careful as he sat down to play cards. His wrist hurt; it was badly swollen. He had not been expecting the brothers' wicked anger at having been outwitted by Slocum's crossing the KC at Coyote Ford instead of where they had anticipated. And yet the news that Slocum—John Slocum—was whipsawing the herd had brought guffaws of pleasure from the group, and they all looked forward to their brother Gans's reaction to the news.

"Glad to join you boys," Dutch said, putting a good face on things; but the aggressive tone of Porky gave his own words a careful ring.

Porky's thick fingers shuffled expertly and he began to deal. "You got money, have you?" He didn't deign to raise his eyes to look at Dutch Dillman as he spoke.

"That I do. And—uh—if I need more, there's my pay coming to me." He dropped a wooden laugh out of his dry mouth as Porky's big hands suddenly stopped in mid-shuffle and he sat there looking at the backs of the cards. Then, cutting his eye slyly at his brother Finn, seated to his left, Porky continued to deal, humming a little song just on his breath.

Dutch Dillman felt a shiver run along his spine. He was beginning to wish that he and Box had not agreed to split up in order to speed their news.

The players were six; and Print, pouring whiskey, announced that it was soon to be a special occasion when Gans arrived, for they would be together in anticipation of brother Goose, who had left the prison in Folsom, California and would be joining them somewhere along the way. Goose LeFort had been away from the action for quite a spell, and his talents had been sorely missed. All the LeForts were looking forward to his return. They were a close family, especially since Goose's imprisonment and Daddy LeFort's death. And there were a number of things they preferred doing together rather than alone—not only card playing and drinking, but also, as the two females in the adjoining room could well attest, womanizing.

"Kid, we are letting you join us on account of you brought good news," Ollie said as he picked up his cards, and looked across the table at Dillman.

"Might be the Arapahoes killed Slocum by now," Dutch said ingratiatingly as he watched the hard faces of his companions. "He scouts the trail every morning and night. Could've run into some Injuns when he didn't have men backing him."

"They had better not have kilt him!" Ollie snapped.

"The orders," Print suddenly shouted, "is to leave Slocum live. Hurt him, that's all right; but not kill the son of a bitch. That's for Gans. You remember that, Dillman! We are saving Slocum for Gans!" His angry eyes bored right into Dutch, who had been totally unprepared for the outburst.

"But the Injuns wouldn't of known that," Dutch foolishly argued. "Nobody knew that. Me and Box, we didn't know it. How could we? Since you all didn't even know Slocum was around. Not till I just brought it to you." He stared from one to the other of the brothers, puzzled.

"Tough titty that is," Finn declared, studying his cards. "Slocum is for Gans. God help the poor son of a bitch who forgets that." He said it mildly, chuckling half to himself as he finished, with his eyes roaming to the open door of the room where the two girls were working.

Dutch, thinking of how he and Box had planned to call Slocum and out-gun him, felt a cold shadow passing through him. At that moment his injured arm gave a bad twinge and his thoughts turned to how he would get even with Slocum. Later. Somehow. Because, to hell with Gans and his brothers. He, Dillman, owed Slocum more than a man could carry for too long.

Dutch, watching his cards, was also able to make some observations regarding the brothers. All of the brothers were big, all were glowering, and all were heavily armed, each carrying a brace of sixguns plus a pigsticker. All also wore galluses as well as wide belts. And Dutch, bringing out his money for the game, suddenly remembered the story he'd heard about some drummer or town slicker one time funning Ollie in the Little Horn Saloon, telling how he had to be pretty damn unsure of himself on account of requiring a belt *and* galluses to hold his pants up. And said it funny, like a friendly joke.

But Ollie had pulled out his pigsticker swift as smoke and without any how-de-do had sliced through that drummer's own galluses and his trousers fell right down around his ankles, pinning him right there. Then Print, who was also present, pulled out his hogleg and told that drummer by jingo to dance. Why, the poor son of a bitch was hopping like a turpentined cat with his pants down around his legs, not able to dance but a couple of hops before he fell down.

Then Print had said, reloading, "You tired, mister?"

The drummer was scared white and fumbling around

on the floor; he was shaking. And he said yes, he was tired.

And Print had said, "Then you better get some sleep, sir." And he'd shot him dead.

They played a few easy hands and then Finn picked up the deck. Finn wore a patch over one eye, having been blinded when a baby pig kicked him when he was not much bigger himself. Daddy LeFort had shot that little animal to hell pronto with a cut-down Greener twelve-gauge, making, as the boys never tired of telling it, a crowd out of that fucking pig. And by God them blue whistlers fixed it so "that piglet never lived to squeal about it!" The joke had been told God knows how many times through the years. The boys were clannish, no matter how you sliced it.

"Straight draw," Finn announced. He dealt quickly, bending his head slightly for better vision, not only at the backs of the other players' cards, but often at the front as well.

Print opened the pot with a pair of jacks, and Finn didn't stay. On the third deal Ollie opened for ten dollars, the usual, on a pair of aces. He was sitting to Finn's left. Finn raised him twenty dollars. Ollie stayed and drew three cards.

Ollie's poker face couldn't last; it turned into a wicked grin. He belched and said, "I play these."

Ollie didn't help the aces. He knew what was coming, but he didn't know how much he would bet. Finn glanced at Ollie's chips, calculating how much he had left.

Finn bet fifty dollars.

Ollie pretended to hesitate. "I call," he said, and spread his hand, face up, showing two aces.

Finn couldn't conceal a look of utter disbelief. "I'll be buggered," he declared, and threw his hand face down in the discards. "Didn't you know I stood pat?" he said in disgust. "How the fuck can you call a pat hand on two aces, for Christ's sake!"

Ollie grinned. "It was my pleasure," he said.

"Go fuck yourself!"

"That's a helluva thing to ask your brother to do."

And all chuckled at this little exchange.

Finn grinned at brother Ollie, lowering his good eyelid slightly. Ollie got up and changed places with Print so that he sat at Finn's left as he dealt. He had got Finn's signal that they were going to strip the kid, who was sitting to his right.

The plan was for Ollie to do the stripping. Several rounds passed before the opportunity came.

"Let's play draw," Finn said. He dealt deliberately, but not slowly, his hands almost hiding each card, while Dillman tried to follow.

Ollie passed. Ike, Print, and Porky passed, making four in all. Dillman, the fifth player, opened with a ten-dollar bet. Finn came out with a twenty-dollar raise. Ollie called. Finn showed no irritation at this, though Ollie knew his brother hadn't planned for more than one player to draw against him. Dillman called, which was according to Finn's plan.

Ollie drew one card.

"Gonna win, are ya?" Finn said.

Olllie didn't answer.

Dillman took three cards. He looked up suddenly and caught Ike LeFort watching him closely, and smiled weakly. He was thinking how the LeFort boys gave a man less room than you could find in an outhouse.

Finn said, "I play these," meaning he was standing pat.

Dutch Dillman, after a quick, nervous look at his cards, checked.

Without a moment's hesitation, Finn bet fifty dollars.

Ollie knew his brother was figuring that he, Ollie, had backed in the pot and was drawing to a straight or a flush. Ollie knew—having been well trained by Daddy, as they all had been—never to risk money drawing one card to a straight or a flush unless there was at least six times the amount of the bet in the pot.

When Finn bet fifty dollars, Ollie raised him a hundred. He didn't have a thing, but he knew his brother was bluffing. He was sure Finn was standing pat on a bust. Dillman didn't matter, having checked. Even if he had helped his hand he would hesitate to call, with Ollie taking one card and raising.

Dutch Dillman showed his openers, two queens, and folded. Finn shook his head, sighing, and threw in his hand. "Imagine drawing one card with all that money riding."

Ollie tossed his hand in the discards and drew in the pot quickly, an angelic expression of innocence on his face.

"I need a drink." Ike stood up, reaching for the bottle. He shot his eyes to the door of the adjoining room. "An' I'm gettin' hungry."

"For what?" laughed Print.

"By God, it makes a man feel good just to think of that," Porky said.

"Whyn't we stop thinking and start doing?" said Finn, scratching himself gently in the crotch.

It was just then that they all heard the horse whicker outside and the guard called through the door, "Gans coming."

In a moment the door opened and Big Gans LeFort stomped in, entering with such size and force that for a moment it seemed his very entrance would overturn the room.

"Ain't that a hot one," he boomed. "Dinwiddie *and* Slocum in the same pot!"

"We wuz appreciatin' that, Gans," Porky said. "And meanwhile we wuz also thinking of having us a little bit of good old poon-tanging!" And, glancing at the open door of the other room, his face lit up and he burst into a great roar of laughter. Instantly, the others took it up, and in a minute the room was rocking with their uncontrollable mirth.

It was a while before they fell away from it, gasping, sucking air, belching and scratching, red-faced and wet-lipped.

Gans reached for the bottle. "Calls for a celebration. But first..." He held up the bottle. "First we are going to drink to Daddy." He threw the bottle to Ike, who caught it and poured into his cup, then tossed the bottle to Finn. And the bottle was tossed, sometimes thrown, to each in turn, a LeFort ritual. Dutch, unprepared, almost dropped the bottle. His hands were shaking as he poured, but his anger at his own fear steadied him.

Gans held his cup high. "This here is to Daddy, on account of we are going to settle it with that son of a bitch Dinwiddie!"

All drank, including Dutch Dillman.

Then Porky lifted his cup. "And this one is for brother Gans, who is going to settle it with that fucking Slocum!"

All drank, gasping and smacking into a moment of silence.

"I do believe Daddy LeFort would of been real proud of us boys," Gans said.

Porky banged his tin cup on the table. "God damn it! Let's get on with it!" And he picked up the deck of cards, raising his voice so the two girls would be sure to hear.

"High cut gets first licks!" He looked around at the others, then turned suddenly to Dillman. "You best get your ass outta here, kid. You ain't kin!"

Dutch Dillman didn't need any urging. He downed his drink and made it swiftly to the door, their loud laughter following.

Dutch didn't go far. He'd had enough to drink to whip up a certain kind of courage, and besides, he hadn't had a woman in a long time. Emboldened by liquor and desire, he circled the cabin and took up a position at one of the back windows, where he could have a good view of the festivities within.

From a high hill Slocum watched Heavy Pete O'Hay riding his favorite chuck wagon mule as the KC herd moved slowly across the open prairie. He'd give it another two days, then they'd have to switch back to night drives. By now the LeForts would surely know from Wagner and Dillman—if not the Arapahoes— that the herd had already crossed the Red River at Coyote Ford. They would also know that it was John Slocum who had slickered them. He could imagine Gans receiving the news. But that was all part of the deal. The future action with Gans made all that much more interesting.

The important point was that for the moment he and Dinwiddie had gained more time by cutting up toward the Cheyenne and Arapaho country. This time the LeForts would expect them at Rabbit Creek, which would be the way Dillman and Wagner would tell it.

Slocum had arranged that, letting Wagner overhear

him telling Dinwiddie that after crossing the Red at Coyote Ford they'd drive directly to Rabbit Creek.

A head start, he reflected ruefully, and maybe a finish. They couldn't keep dodging the LeForts forever. At some point there would have to be a confrontation. The thing was for him to choose the time and place, not the LeForts. He'd give them three days to cut the new trail. And again his thoughts ran over the men, the guns, the ammunition.

Dinwiddie's crew was down from a dozen to ten, not counting Slocum. There were six LeForts, and who knew how many hired guns. Dinwiddie had reckoned another half-dozen. The LeFort brothers didn't like to take unnecessary chances, he realized. But the LeForts were not the only problem, nor were the Indians or the weather. There was the girl and her uncle.

He had talked to the girl about it the night before.

"We will take you as far as Medicine Bluff," he'd told her.

She had looked up at him with a gaze of complete innocence. "Where is that?"

"A good way from here. But it's before we get too deep into Cheyenne and Arapaho country. And it's close to one of the wagon trails. And there's an agent there."

"Agent?"

"The Indian agent. He'll advise you how to go on."

"But I thought the Indians were at peace."

"That's what the piece of paper says. But not all the Indians can read. Nor can a good many whites, it seems."

They had been taking a walk out by the remuda after supper. He had asked her to accompany him after the Reverend had conducted a service and Ava had played the small organ which they had lifted down from the Conestoga. She had passed out hymnals and everyone sang. Slocum had enjoyed it, though it was not something he would wish to repeat every night.

"But you said you were going on to Abilene," she said. "Can't we go along with you? That sounds like a good place for Uncle Miller to spread his work."

He looked down at her. She wasn't a short girl, but he was over six feet and she came to just above his shoulder. A good size, he was thinking as he looked along the edge of her cheek. She was wearing a riding skirt now and a printed blouse which did little to hide the contour of her superb bust. Slocum had difficulty taking his eyes off her as she spoke questioningly to him. "We have been told many times that the Indians were all peaceful on the reservations."

"True. They're supposed to be," he had replied. "Only now and again some of the young bucks like to take off for some fun—stealing horses..." He grinned at her. "Stealing girls."

"I can take care of myself," she said, and he caught the crispness in her tone.

He half felt, half watched from the corner of his eye the frown that had come into her face, and he turned to look directly at her again. He decided right then and there that she was just as good-looking when she was frowning as when she was smiling. It didn't matter what kind of expression she wore, as far as he was concerned. She was delightful.

Only what was she doing out here in the wilderness with a preacher uncle, playing the organ, singing hymns, and without a man? He couldn't understand it. But he was intrigued. Ava Muldoon was just about the best-looking woman he'd seen since ever.

"If you'd let us go on with you... well, we don't have any money to pay you, but I could work. I can do the men's laundry. I can do chores. I can help with the cooking."

He threw back his head and laughed outright. And his laughter was so contagious she joined him.

"I really don't know what's so funny," she said when they subsided. Her eyes were dancing over his face.

"I can't imagine Heavy Pete allowing you to come in on his cooking."

"Heavy Pete? That big man? Oh, I can get around him."

They had stopped walking and stood together quietly now. He was grinning at her sureness, her confidence in her attractiveness. By God, she had plenty to be confident about, he reflected as he felt his desire rise.

"I'm sure you can get around him, or any man in the outfit. But that's not the point." He let his face turn serious. "I'm responsbile for this drive, for getting the cattle to the pens in Abilene. But I have no intention of taking on the responsibility for you and your uncle."

"I don't really understand."

"We're going to be coming up against some rough action. You could get hurt. And your uncle, too. He isn't a young man."

"But the Indians are at peace. Even you have said so."

"I'm sorry."

"But..." She had turned her fawn-like eyes fully upon him and he thought his heart would swell right out of his chest.

"No buts," he said.

"I've a feeling you're not telling me the whole story," she said. "Is it because I'm a woman and you—you're a big, strong frontiersman?" And she tilted her head to one side, biting her lower lip gently as her eyes gazed over his face.

Slocum couldn't stand it. "By golly, a man sure wouldn't need a stove in the winter being around you, young lady."

Her laughter was like a handful of little bells.

"You look at me like that, Miss Muldoon, and you're going to find yourself in trouble. I promise you."

Total innocence swept through every fiber of her face and body. "I'm sure I don't know what you mean, Mr. Slocum. Find myself... in trouble?"

"You'll find yourself on your back. Is that better?"

She was standing facing him with her hands clasped lightly behind her, one foot slightly outstretched, as she rotated her heel on a little mound of dirt. Straightening now, she said, "Well, thank you for the walk. I must get back to Uncle Miller. He has to take his medicine, and he invariably forgets." And she smiled with her eyes glowing at him and suddenly ran back to the Conestoga wagon.

Slocum had stood there watching after her. It was some good while before his passion subsided. She had disappeared into the wagon, and he waited a few moments, but she didn't come out. Half aloud he had said, "I am still leaving you and the Reverend at Medicine Bluff, Miss Muldoon, God damn it!"

He forced thoughts of the girl away from him now and rode over the crown of the hill, dropping down the side away from the cattle. It didn't take him long to quarter down to the rolling land where the grass was belly-deep to his horse, and he could see that the deer were plentiful. But this time he shot some quail and packed the tasty meat into camp.

That night Slocum found himself again wondering about the girl. He had a definite feeling that she wasn't really all that religious. Her body was much too lovely for a life of celibacy or devotion to spiritual matters. So what was she doing out here in the middle of nowhere, singing hymns and praying with her aged uncle?

Slocum had to give up on it. It was some mystery. But he knew one thing; that he was surely going to find out the answer.

6

At Rabbit Creek tempers were warm. The LeForts and their cadre of gunmen had arrived in high anticipation, looking for signs of Slocum and Dinwiddie and the KC herd. But only moments later they saw that once again they had been foiled. There was not a sign of the cattle having passed or of their impending arrival.

"Well, where the fuck are they?" Gans swung hard out of the saddle, ground-hitched his big, dappled gray horse and glared at Dillman and Wagner, who were already afoot, looking for a trail to follow.

"You're not gonna find it in those goddamn bushes, for Christ's sake!" snarled Ike.

Ollie spat furiously in the direction of the two failed spies. "Jesus, we're gonna have to ride all the way back to where you two assholes left 'em and cut their back trail!"

Gans was white around the lips, his onyx-colored eyes like stones of anger. "Of course, Slocum figgered you two pair of shits would tell us they'd be crossing Rabbit Creek here. You went and swallowed just what they told you!"

"But we never..." Wagner said hotly, his wet-looking face more damp than ever. "They didn't tell us nothing. I overheard him telling it to Dinwiddie. He never told me an' Dutch nothing. That's how we figgered it was the truth."

"They must've changed their plan after we left," Dillman said.

"Stupid! Fucking stupid!" roared Gans. "Fall for the oldest trick in the book, old with hair on it; stupid, stinking like you with stupid! Overheard them! Jesus Christ, a damn five-year-old would know better'n that! You know that son of a bitch Slocum's got Injun in him. Slickered you quicker'n you can wet yer pants, for Christ's sake!"

"Ought to leave the two of them right out here stripped, Gans. What do you think?" Ollie had drawn his sixgun and was twirling it in his hand.

But Gans was studying on it, pursing his thoughts in deep concentration. "Anger don't help right now," he said as he squatted.

The brothers followed suit, hunkering at the edge of a buffalo wallow, making a grim semicircle. Meanwhile four non-family members, not counting Dillman and Wagner, led their horses to the creek.

"They can't be too far away," said Gans, "even so. You can't hide a whole herd of Texas longhorns so easy like." His eyes were on Dillman and Wagner.

"Shit!" exclaimed Finn.

"Easy now." Gans, usually the first to anger, generally turned calm the moment the others had lost their tempers. It was always a good way to control things. "Easy now," he went on. "Just remember how Daddy used to put it, that you can catch more flies going slow than racing about." He had kept his deadly eyes right on Wagner and Dillman while he was speaking. "Now you boys," he continued, purring the words. "You two young boys, suppose, just suppose like you had two thousand head of cow stuff and you wanted to get 'em up to Kansas in the worst way. How would you go, eh?"

Dillman, looking for a trap, saw none, but Gans's quiet was more frightening than his rage. "I'd head them straight north, but keeping away from the Indian Territory."

"Uh-huh. You would? You sure?"

"Sure I'm sure." Those eyes were still on him, holding him. He had to resist the urge to jump to his feet and draw, but he knew if he did he was a dead man. He felt sweat dripping down around his collar.

"And you..." The black stones turned to Box Wagner.

"The same," Box said.

"Sure?"

"I am sure." And Dutch Dillman could see his companion biting his lower lip.

"Then you've got a second chance," Gans said. "Find them!"

Nobody moved after those words were spoken. The tableau by the buffalo wallow was frozen.

Porky was the first to make a gesture. He raised his head. "Get on and get out," he said. "And it ain't your second chance, it's your last!"

When the pair were gone, Gans spun on his brother. "You control yourself, brother, when I have got a play going!"

"Go fuck yerself, Gans. You're not talking to John Slocum now."

Almost before the words were out of Porky's mouth, Gans had backhanded him in the throat, knocking him off balance. In a trice both were on their feet, and Gans knocked his brother to his knees with a wicked punch in the side of his neck and, as he was going down, brought his knee up right underneath Porky's chin.

"Christ, Gans!" The words broke from Finn Le-Fort.

"You disagree, Finn boy?"

"Nope. But you might've kilt him."

"I didn't. Drag him to the creek and see."

Ollie and Print and Finn all carried their unconscious brother to the creek and revived him by dunking him in the cold water.

When Porky finally staggered back to the group at the buffalo wallow, Gans said, "That's for anybody who makes a crack about me and Slocum. Remember it!"

Porky had a strange grin on his face. "I owe you one, Gans."

"I'll be waiting." Gans spat hard at a clump of fresh horse manure, then looked up at the horizon.

"Jesus, Gans, you like to broke my goddamn neck." Porky had bent his head and was rubbing his neck with the palms of both hands.

"I fucked up, didn't I?" And this sally brought a guffaw of laughter from the group.

And Gans, full of high good spirits, reached over and slapped his brother on the back and, putting his arm around him, hugged him hard. "Let's drink to it, by God!"

Ike reached into his saddlebag, brought out a bottle, and uncorked it.

"Porky first," said Gans. "By God, he earned it!" He swung on the others. "Well, ain't it the way Daddy did it? You forgot, have you? Didn't he beat the shit out of us since the day we was borned, and didn't it learn us?"

They were all silent in the face of the truth of Gans's statement regarding their father. "You recollect," Gans went on, "when we wuz shavers, you never knew when he'd suddenly knock you right across the room, or come up behind and cold-cock you just for not being alert and watching. By God, he trained us, he did!"

"Said you had to be watching all the time," Finn eagerly agreed. "Huh! I mind the time I had my hands full roaching that crazy white mare's mane down on the cotton farm and Daddy snuck up on her off side—she wuz blind in that eye, by God—an' he spooked the shit out of her. Wham! I went ass over teakettle. Broke a rib, a couple of knuckles. An' he bawled the shit out of me for not watchin'!"

As the evening slipped into the little clearing they sat there at the buffalo wallow drinking and reminiscing, each one with a story to tell about their irascible parent, while the four gunmen took sentry duty.

"He sure wasn't soft, you can say that," Ollie recalled with a grin. "Why, I don't ever recollect him being soft, not with any of us. That right?"

They nodded. Then Ike spoke up. "I remember oncet."

"You're full of shit."

"No, by God! Daddy, he give me a pat on the back of my head one time. I took it to mean I did something he liked."

"Jesus!" Print let out a small whoop of disbelief. "What did you do to get that?"

"I was like fifteen," Ike said. "And I had a real nice little Mexican gal, and I let Daddy have her one time. And after, he give me that pat on the head."

The story brought another round of appreciative laughter as they continued to address the bottle of whiskey, and presently they opened another one. The stories were all endlessly familiar, but maybe that was why they enjoyed them so much. It was good to know what was going to happen.

And then at one point, with all of them well loosened, Porky passed the bottle to Gans, not throwing it this time, but handing it; and just as his brother reached for it, he dropped it and brought his elbow around to smash Gans a solid wallop right on his ear. But Gans rolled with it, robbing it of its force. And he just sat there laughing. And finally, drying his eyes with the backs of his hands, weak with laughter, he managed to get the words out. "See, Porky, I was ready for you! I let you get even, and it didn't hurt me none. You get it, boy? You get it?"

There had been no sign of the LeForts, nor of Little Coyote and his Arapahoes. Slocum had pushed the herd hard, covering good ground, although it was difficult, due to their having to make their own trail. Now the game was scanty and they had fallen back on Heavy Pete's staples: sourdough biscuits, sowbelly bacon, molasses, brown Mexican beans, and black jawbreaker coffee.

Slocum had said nothing further to the Muldoons about leaving the herd at Medicine Bluff. Dinwiddie had agreed completely with his decision. "They'll hold us down in a fracas," was how the cattleman put it. "And that nice, pretty gal—we don't want her getting in all that trouble."

Slocum still felt the mystery of what Ava was doing out in the middle of the prairie with an organ, a bunch of hymnals, and her uncle. Everything about her proclaimed a different life. And at times he even felt the same way about the Reverend. Had he perhaps been kicked out of his church back East? Perhaps for favoring the booze; for, indeed, he had noticed that the

Reverend Muldoon, while preaching strenuously against the bottle, nevertheless partook of it with vigor. No, there had to be more to it than that; for, in that case, why would the girl be with him?

Something refused to come to the front of his mind. And so he waited, knowing from experience that sooner or later it would work itself through. Or there would be a revealing word spoken, a gesture, if he watched carefully and waited.

One morning the point rider reported a small herd of buffalo in a pocket valley to the east.

"Nice to make a change to venison, wouldn't you say?" Slocum put it to Dinwiddie.

"You'll take the Sharps?"

"Like to try her out again."

"And can you take me?" said the voice coming up behind them. "I overheard the point rider telling Pete about the buffalo. Couldn't I come along, please? I have never seen a real live buffalo."

She was standing there in her split riding skirt, and this time wearing a lemon-colored silk shirt, open at the throat. Looking as neat as a bandbox, Slocum thought; and somehow delightfully out of breath.

"You'll have to keep out of the way," he said gruffly.

"I wasn't asking to shoot the animal, Mr. Slocum, only to watch how you do it."

He couldn't fail to hear the teasing tone in her voice, and he felt something race with pleasure inside him. At the same time, he was determined to maintain a discipline and distance with both her and her uncle, if he had any hope of getting them to leave the drive at Medicine Bluff. He knew what she was trying. And she was damn good at it.

"Come along, then," he said.

The little valley wasn't far, and they reached it shortly, coming in downwind from the grazing animals.

"Not a very big herd," he said, as he and the girl watched from the slope of a low hill. "But we only need one good cow."

There were some thirty to forty in the herd, and now Slocum edged his horse down toward them.

"Won't they see us?" the girl asked, almost in a whisper.

"They can't see far. But they can smell." He drew rein and they sat their horses a moment.

"I thought that, you know. I thought that was why we came in toward them from downwind."

"You're bright," he said, and he meant it, but he saw her reaction.

"Thank you, and so are you—bright," she said in a brittle tone. And then flashed a wicked smile at him. Then almost immediately she said, "I'm sorry. I get nasty sometimes."

"What do you do about that?" he asked.

Her smile was even more wicked. "Get nastier."

Slocum regarded her coolly for a long moment, not moving his eyes from her face. He said nothing.

Finally she shifted in her saddle. "I really am sorry, you know."

"In this country a man can get shot for less."

"Will you forgive me? I didn't mean it like that. I was...playing. I guess I'm pretty upset about this Medicine Bluff place, or whatever it's called."

"No. I won't forgive you."

"That's mean. I said I didn't mean it."

"You meant it, or you wouldn't have said it. In this country, Miss Muldoon, there is no forgiveness. Remember that if you want to stay alive."

She didn't say anything, and he stepped down from his horse.

"We've got a good three hundred yards," he said.

And after a moment she asked, "Will they run away when you start shooting?"

"Not if I do it right."

Looking at the meager herd, he remembered Yellow Eagle the Arapaho chief some years ago on the Washita telling him that soon there would be no longer any buffalo. And he could still see in his mind the sorrow in the chief's face as he spoke. He had wanted to say something then, but he hadn't.

Now he cut a quick glance at Ava. Her mood had changed completely and her gray eyes were sparkling with excitement as she watched the great shaggy beasts.

"I've never even imagined they could be like this!"

He had taken out the Sharps and was checking its load. It was a hefty weapon, a .50-.70 with a beautiful balance, and power. He had felt it firing at the Indians the other day.

"I'll use those buffalo sticks," he said.

She handed them to him almost eagerly.

He started walking slowly toward the grazing animals and she followed only a step or two behind.

Stopping, he knelt on one knee and, handing her the rifle, opened the buffalo sticks. They were made of bois d'arc, or Osage orange, each about three feet long, and riveted together near one end, so that they were able to swing open like a pair of big shears.

He took the rifle from her now, placed the barrel in the upper crotch, and held both sticks and the barrel with his left hand.

"I thought you shot buffalo lying down on the ground or from a horse," she said. "I read that somewhere, I think."

"I'll need to be closer," he said after sighting, not responding to her observation.

Now they moved to about two hundred yards from the grazing herd. And he again set up the buffalo sticks and rested the barrel of the Sharps on them.

"If you shoot lying down they'll feel the vibration running along the ground and they'd likely stampede," he told her.

"I see."

At last he singled out an old cow. Aiming carefully, he squeezed off a shot, holding for the lungs. He watched the impact and, as he had expected, the cow kept her feet.

"You missed," the girl said, again almost whispering.

"Shut up."

He watched the cow bleeding and waited until the other animals, smelling the blood, began to mill around the wounded cow.

"You watch this, Miss Smart-pants," he said, settling himself in line with his sighting.

This time he shot for the neck of a big bull. The shot was clean, the animal dropping where it stood. Then he shot a second buffalo, also with a single bullet.

Slocum rose to his feet, and after a moment let his eyes turn from the herd to the girl beside him, who was staring in amazement with her mouth slightly open.

"Understand now why I hit the cow?" he said.

"Yes—yes, I see."

"Heavy Pete can help us skin and butcher them," he said.

And for a moment as he stood there looking at her he forgot about the LeForts, the herd, the buffalo, and felt only the fact of their being there together and alone.

"We'll have meat for a good while," he said.

"They're getting played out," Gans was saying. "Time they get to the Canadian they'll be easy pickings. I mean except that son of a bitch, Slocum," he added quickly.

"He's a goddamn sharpshooter," Porky said, with a careful glance at his brother. "They say he can shoot the asshole right out of a running prairie dog."

"When we get through with him—When Gans gets through with him, is what I am meaning," Finn added hurriedly, "he won't be fit to shoot hisself."

They were sitting their horses in the shade of a cutbank. It was close to noon. Nearby, two Arapaho braves from Little Coyote's band waited.

They had delivered their message, telling the location of the herd. No, they had not seen the two white men sent by Gans. But the man Slocum had sighted them before they could look further, and he had fired and chased them. He had a big thunderstick. Very loud.

"Likely a Sharps," Ike said.

"You go back to Little Coyote," Gans instructed. "Tell him we want the cattle stampeded."

"Little Coyote want more whiskey, burning water."

They stood patiently while the brothers conferred, Gans as usual doing the leading.

"Tell Little Coyote he'll get whiskey when they get the cattle stampeded," Gans said to Porky.

His brother repeated it, making signs.

"They understand?" Gans spat angrily. "They sure don't look it."

"Where is the leader, the one with one feather?" Ike asked.

"Little Coyote is waiting for them near the river," Porky said. He turned to Gans. "They say they'll tell Little Coyote about the stampeding."

"They don't look happy about it," Finn declared loudly.

"Better give 'em a bottle," Ike said.

Gans snapped, "Then the buggers'll just sit around and get stiff." He waved his hands at the two Indians. "Go on! Git!"

Sullenly the two scouts turned and jumped onto their ponies, and in a moment they were gone.

Gans glared after them, then turned to his brothers. "Where the fuck is them two what was s'posed to locate the KC?"

"Maybe took off," suggested Ollie.

Print slipped his right foot out of his stirrup, swung his leg up onto the pommel of his saddle, and sat there at his ease. "Gans, why don't we just move in now and take them? Shit, we wait around here—what for? I'm tired of this waiting. We outgun them a good two to one."

"Better," put in Finn.

But Gans was already shaking his big head. "You want to live to dip yer wick again, boy?"

"You mean Slocum?" Porky watched for his brother's reaction.

Gans's face darkened. They all noted it. And they left a careful silence for him to speak.

"I have told you knotheads," he began slowly, "and told you again...that we don't want no slipups. I want a complete rubout. We have spent one helluva lot of time and money stopping these Texas herds.

And, by God, we got other things to do. We spend all our time fighting the Texans, we'll lose the market. This has got to be the last one... the convincer."

"That's just what I'm saying," roared Finn. "Let's get shut of the bastards oncet for all!"

"My way," Gans said softly. "It'll be my way. We—I—got to choose how we'll settle Slocum."

"And Dinwiddie," put in Print.

"And Dinwiddie. But without no slipups. That Slocum is slicker'n a fucking coyote. I know. I got to admit he slickered me; not by strength, but dirty like. Fighting real dirty. Yeah! Next time I'll be ready for him!" He sniffed loudly, and belched, and his voice grew as he warmed to himself. "Remember—don't *never* forget it—I want him for myself! Got that? And the herd wiped out! Not the cattle! The men, you asshole!" he whipped out at Ollie, as he saw his brother opening his mouth to speak.

Gans raised his thick forefinger aloft, and only his head moved as he eyeballed each of his brothers.

"And Dinwiddie," Porky said. "We'll all of us count coup on Dinwiddie."

"That is the way Daddy would've wanted it."

"And Goose!" Print cut in. "Goose'll want in on it; that's a gut!"

"Where the hell is Goose?" Ollie wanted to know. "About due, ain't he?"

"I left word at Red River Station," Gans said. "But you can't tell. Coming from California like that, he might be slowed down some." And he added, "Goose will not want to miss this one." He leaned forward now onto the pommel of his saddle, his forearms crossed, hunching his shoulders, gripping each of his brothers with his eyes in turn. "We will do 'er like this. We'll hold back, see. Play it easy, like we been doing it. Let them beat themselves. The storm, that surely hurt them. And the Injuns. They'll do some more stampeding. Keep 'em off balance. See, they thought they gained time crossing at Coyote Ford, but that big storm beat 'em. Didn't cost us a damn thing. See what I mean?" And he looked around at each one of them, laughing. "And we'll just nudge 'em like that. Stampede, run off their horses, drygulch one or two..." He paused, working the fingers of his right hand. "Whiskey the Indians a good bit, that'll trouble them. And..." He paused again, a sly grin stealing into his face. And we'll see..." The grin spread.

After a moment someone said, "But Coyote, he's lost some men."

"So he will likely lose some more."

"Only thing is, that could cool him off," Ollie pointed out.

"Give him more whiskey, then."

"The thing is, we don't want his tribe coming down on him," cautioned Porky. "Least not till we're shut of him. I hear that Yellow Eagle is tough on the drinking and raiding."

"Coyote pays no mind to that."

"He's liable to get his throat slitted if the chief gets wind of it, is all."

"That," said Gans, "will be for him to handle. Not us."

"What I am saying," Porky insisted, "is that Yellow Eagle, if he catches on, could have the whole tribe jumping on *our* ass."

But his brother Gans was shaking his head. "No. No. Now, here is the way it is going to be. We will wait till they cross the Canadian, if they get that far. By then they'll have been on the trail one helluva long time, and they will be tired and then they'll start making mistakes." He waited a moment. "Good idea! We'll have Coyote and his boys poke them more at night. Don't let 'em rest. Keep 'em on their guard day and night. Get it? They'll be so tired they won't know whether they're riding or taking a piss!" He stopped, grinning again. "And we'll be waiting at the Canadian." His eyes narrowed. *"I'll* be waiting," he said softly. And he was the only one who heard it.

Little Coyote led his band of less than a dozen braves up the slope of a wide coulee, heading toward some mesquite trees. From here it was possible to sweep the long, wide land with the white man's far-seeing glass.

"There!" spoke Charging Thunder, who was squatting beside his cousin, with his eyes pressed to the strong eyes.

Little Coyote took the army field glasses. "The cow animals," he said.

"And the cow men."

Little Coyote lowered the glasses and looked at his small band. They had painted their bodies with green lightning stripes and white hail spots. Two of them still had pains in the head and stomach from the white man's stinging water. But they were coming round. They were all young men and they were feeling restive—impatient and eager for action.

"I hope that we are not followed," Charging Thunder said, and he turned his head to the two braves who had come up to them.

"We will not be followed," Little Coyote was saying. "Our tracks were silent and are no longer where we passed." And he looked at Walks Silently and Falling Star, who were bringing news from the gray men.

"The gray men want us to run-away the cows," Walks Silently said.

"Did they give you any of the whiskey?"

"No, they said we would have some after we made the cows run-away."

"And what of thundersticks? And ammunition? Bullets and powder? We have need of everything. Not the whiskey," Little Coyote said, looking angrily at his cousin Charging Thunder.

"They said they had no more guns and bullets to spare for us," Falling Star answered. "They want us to follow the cow men to the north, to the river they call Canada. Then there will be guns."

"Canadian River. It is not very far; but it is not the Canada that is Grandmother's Country. What will they do there?"

"They want us to follow and wait. But first the run-away. Then we will meet them there and will tell them what we see."

"We must be careful," Charging Thunder said. "We will be close to Yellow Eagle's camp."

"He will not know we are near," a young man named Hog Talking said. "It will be safe."

"How not?" Little Coyote replied sharply. "Yellow Eagle always has many scouts in the country. He knows everything that happens. He could even know that we are here."

"Yellow Eagle sometimes acts like a blanket chief," said a brave named Turtle, and seeing the anger flashing in Little Coyote's eyes he said quickly, "I mean no disrespect."

"You never speak so!" Little Coyote said angrily to Turtle's bowed head. And his hand dropped to his pony whip.

After a moment Charging Thunder said, "I wish

we were more warriors." And his eyes studied the tiny band.

Little Coyote said, "But when we are few, the pony soldiers do not trouble themselves to chase us."

Little Coyote stood up. He was a lean, lightly muscled young man with long black hair hanging on his shoulders. The scar along his right jaw had come from a grizzly bear with whom he had fought only a few years before when he was still a boy. He had killed the bear, and since then he had been honored in the tribe as a young man of great promise. And he had earned the honor to wear one feather. But Little Coyote's pride had also grown with his prowess as a warrior, and he had chafed at remaining so long on the reservation and doing what the white men wanted. And so had his friends, especially his cousin Charging Thunder. Surely they could live a life that was more free.

Yet he regretted the whiskey. For now, even though, like Yellow Eagle, he had ordered that it must not be taken, there were those who disobeyed. And with the gray men promising to get them guns, and giving them whiskey, he was caught. For the guns were needed, and the young men to fire them. Right now they could shoot only a few bullets, and these were weak in powder.

Mounting his pony, Little Coyote signaled that they would ride north and west, just ahead of the cows. In that way they could annoy the cow men, the way the man Gans and the other gray men wanted. Until the meeting at the big river called Canadian.

And as they rode now in single file with Charging Thunder directly behind him, Little Coyote was thinking that it was good; for listening to the restlessness of the riders behind, he knew that they were growing angry—as he was—and would be ready to run-away the cows and fight the white cow men if need be.

In a few moments now he would order them to be quiet so that they would hold their impatience and anger and not spend it in idle gossip and bragging and in unnecessary movement. Then they would have the force for fighting. They could then behave as warriors. And maybe soon he could stop the whiskey.

It seemed the brilliance of the dying day would always be there; and the yellow flowers and the bluebirds with the slanting sunlight on their wings. Slocum listened to the myriad sounds from the earth and the animals; the rustling of the leaves as the wind stirred along the creek, the swishing of their horses' tails chasing away the flies, the dry ticking of the meadow as the day ended.

"Medicine Bluff is the other side of that tableland," he said. He was standing swing-hipped, looking down at the corner of her eye where it met her high cheekbone.

"We don't want to go." She was looking across the meadow. "Uncle is just as much against it as I am."

"I've told both of you that you can't stay with us. That it isn't safe."

"I know. I'm sorry. I still don't understand why." She turned to face him fully, holding her hand above her eyes as though shading them, though there was no need to.

He watched the swell of her breasts as her breath seemed to catch on her words.

"I've told you. I'm expecting big trouble up near the Canadian River. You can get hurt, killed even. There'll be a lot of gunfighting."

"What you're really saying is we'll be in the way. Isn't that what you mean? That's what you're afraid of, isn't it?"

"You'll be in the way, yes; and, like I said, you can be shot, scalped, raped, tortured. Who knows what? I'm not just talking about Indians. I'm talking about the men who are doing their damnedest to break up this herd and keep us out of Kansas. They'll kill all of us if necessary. I mean it!"

"Yes, of course." She sounded weary. "Uncle and I talked it over after you spoke to him last night. But he said, 'Isn't it better dying together with friends than alone?' That's how he put it. And we will surely be alone. I mean, after we leave here."

They were silent, and he was thinking of her not being there after the morning came. How long had it been? A week? It didn't matter. Not long, anyway. And yet; long and also not long—both.

She had fitted in so readily with the drive. Helping Heavy Pete, now and then joshing with the riders, getting them coffee, even doing some sewing. The Reverend, for his part, had delivered sermons, written a letter or two for men who didn't know how, and spoken about the place of tiny man in a huge universe, plus the horrors of drink. He was loquacious, interested in the land more than in people, it seemed to Slocum. He had noted early Reverend Muldoon's taste for whiskey. As he put it himself, "Taken medicinally, with good intention, drink drives out bad thoughts." And he had told Slocum how a man of God must know the devil in order to deal with the devil. "Whiskey, after all, Slocum, lubricates the difficult moments of a man's life." And, lifting his glass, "This now is one of those moments, sir. I'm sure you will agree."

He had grown to like the older man, with his wheeze, and his quiet. He seemed content simply to ride on his wagon box and gaze at the passing scenery by the hour without getting the least bit restless. Slocum had watched him at those moments, and had noticed an expression of...fondness was the word that came to him...on Muldoon's doughy face.

One day, when Slocum had ridden up beside the wagon as they were crossing a stretch of rolling prairie, the Reverend had turned his head and said, "All those prayer books, Slocum; what good are they in the face of this?" And he swept his hand in a wide gesture over the land before them. "A man learns nothing from a book, but everything from nature. Nature is the true book." And he turned his smiling eyes to Slocum. "You see, the trouble is, men worship God, and at the same time hate his handiwork. How is that possible?"

The girl shared her uncle's tranquil containment. Yet to Slocum she was still a puzzle. More so than ever, as he watched her talking to the men, doing chores, riding on the wagon seat or on the back of the black gelding. And her attention seemed totally given to her uncle's welfare, without the slightest impatience or resentment. Slocum was touched, but more puzzled than ever.

"Well..." she said now as the sun dropped behind the horizon and a very slight coolness came into the air. "I've done my best to convince you. You're a tough man, Mr. John Slocum."

"You almost succeeded," he said. "I wish I could spare a man to go with you. But it'll be safe. I'll scout ahead early in the morning."

They were silent in the listening of the coming night. And before he knew it darkness had fallen, though her outline was clear standing beside him. And he could feel the pulsing coming from her stronger as the night awakened.

In the next moment he had taken her hand, and together they had walked to the protection of the trees along the side of the creek. And then he had his arms around her and his mouth against hers. Her lips opened with her breath and his tongue found hers, touching tenderly, then probing hungrily, while his hands slipped along the curving undulation of her body. He began undressing her, his fingers slipping along her silken skin, his entire body streaming with joy.

"Oh, my God," she cried softly against his lips, her breath hot with passion. "Oh, John, John, how I've been wanting you, waiting, praying for you!" Her knees buckled, and neither of them could stand another moment, melting to the ground, both undressing frantically.

They lay side by side while her thighs straddled his huge erection, and he played his fingers along her back, her buttocks, and around and into her silky bush to find her lips soaking with readiness.

In a moment he was on top of her and she had spread her legs wide, lifting them now as he came down, then bracing her feet on the ground to receive his long, thick organ, every particle of her sighing in ecstasy.

Now their bodies were undulating slowly, then more quickly as their passion mounted, and he plunged deeper into her, and higher, going as far as he could go, and further it seemed, all but splitting her as she thrust and squirmed, moaning, biting his shoulder, digging her fingers into his pumping buttocks, and finally reaching down to fondle his fully loaded balls.

"John, John, I can't hold it any longer. Oh, oh,

oh, my God, my God, give it to me, please, please... oh, my God!"

And, stroking faster and faster, while he thought he could not hold himself another second, and yet somehow he did as the most exquisite joy grew and grew while their bodies thrashed in perfect rhythmic blending, finally dancing to the ultimate of their desire as they came together.

He lay beside her, his face buried in her neck, while she caressed him weakly, moaning lightly now, murmuring. He was totally empty; clear, clean, his whole body sighing in soft delight.

Presently he began to grow again as she touched him, her fingers exploring, and he became more aware of the delicious aroma of her sex, feeling it still wet on his thighs and belly. His member grew and he began to pump his loins as she stroked his wet shaft. She spread her legs, lying on her back now, and he slipped into her, reaching under her to caress her pumping buttocks. Then she wrapped her legs right around him, grabbed his buttocks, and pulled him savagely to her as they rode faster and faster, then slower, more gently. He drew his long cock almost all the way out of her, not entirely, only to the exquisite last inch, to the very edge of her swollen lips, as she begged him not to leave, clutched him, grabbing his balls to assure his staying. And he slid slowly into her again, wriggling his hips as he held the head of his member tight up inside her, as high and deep as it would go. And again they found their rhythm, riding each other in perfect unison until together they dissolved and lay totally blissful in one another's arms.

They lay beneath the stars until Slocum heard someone calling his name.

She stirred beneath him. "You'd better go."

"I reckon. But I sure don't want to."

"I know."

Somehow they got into their clothes. He waited for her, then watched her walking toward the wagon. She didn't turn around.

Slocum walked toward the man who was calling him. Looking westward where the moon stood on the land, he realized that she would be gone tomorrow and he would never know the answer to her mystery. But he knew he didn't care. He liked her a lot just the way she was.

In the morning Slocum scouted the country toward Medicine Bluff and then he rode back to the chuck wagon and had coffee and sourdough biscuits and molasses with the men. He chatted with Heavy Pete and Dinwiddie. There was no sign of the girl or her uncle. They had said their goodbyes the night before. The wagon was standing where it had been when they made camp, and Slocum was just starting to wonder where the two of them were when Ava appeared. He watched her climb down from the wagon and hitch the team.

Slocum tossed the last of his coffee into the fire and called to the men to mount up. By the time they had the longhorns lined up and moving, the girl and Reverend Muldoon were on their way. It didn't take him long to catch up with them.

The girl was driving, the Reverend seated beside her. When she saw him she pulled the team to a halt. Smiling down at him, she bid him good morning.

"You've got those extra guns and ammo," he said, for want of anything better to say.

"Yes, we do."

He had stopped close beside the wagon, nodding

to the Reverend, and now he pushed the brim of his big hat up so that he could look at the girl on the wagon box more clearly.

"Come to say goodbye."

"Goodbye, Slocum, and we thank you again." The Reverend's face was more lined than usual, it seemed. Slocum thought he didn't look very happy, but he expected that.

"I would offer you coffee," Ava said, "only I expect you have to get back to your charges."

"That is so." And he held her eyes, not wanting to let go.

"A slight dram of the creature, Mister Slocum?" said Reverend Muldoon, transforming suddenly into his former self.

"Thank you, no, Reverend. I got a big day ahead."

"So have we, my boy, and, if you'll excuse me, I shall prepare for it." And he turned and went back into the wagon and out of sight.

Slocum said, "You'd better get going. You'll make it fine."

"That is what I sure reckon," she said, imitating him with a western twang, but there was no humor in it. She was on the point of tears.

She picked up the reins, and he noticed her blue shirt had a little tear at the armpit. How unlike her, he thought. He felt desire thumping in him again. She flicked the lines onto the rumps of the team and, as the wagon started to roll, he turned his pony out of the way, still keeping his eyes on her.

"So long," he said, still holding her with his look.

She turned her head. Her mouth opened slightly. She smiled, a clean little smile. "So short..."

7

"Told you we'd find 'em." Box Wagner dealt the words with a big grin of triumph on his face, as he cut a wink at his pal Dillman.

But Porky LeFort and his brothers were not grinning.

"What the hell you talkin' about! The Araps knew where they were all along, and told us!"

"Did they tell you Slocum's stuck at the Little Wichita on account of the river's over its banks and he can't cross?"

"Yes, they did!" Ike's words whipped their ears, and their faces fell.

Now Gans leaned in. "So!" The single word said more than all the others together. He glared at the two young men who so fancied themselves gunswifts. "The Arapahoes told us that, too. Glad I didn't send you fuckers lookin' for the Fourth of July, for Christ's sake!"

Both Dillman and Wagner took a moment with that. They had arrived at the end of the day where the LeForts were camped in a valley bottom, to be greeted with derision and fury over their incompetence. But the boys still had a card up their sleeve. By now it was overdue.

"Maybe they told you about the wagon, huh?" Dutch, remembering his hatred for Slocum, rallied beneath the glares of the LeForts.

The brothers exchanged glances at that. And now

Box came in, making no effort to keep the triumph out of his voice as he said, "It 'pears they didn't."

"Wagon? What you mean, wagon?"

"We told you two to locate Slocum and Dinwiddie and those cows!" Gans roared suddenly. "Stop this goddamn bullshittin' around! We got the news long ago from the Arap scouts. What the hell you bin doin'? What's all this bullshit about a wagon!"

So great was his anger that even though he remained where he was, not moving forward even an inch, both Dillman and Wagner stepped back.

This time it was Box who rallied. "The wagon with the old preacher man and the girl. They got company. Slocum has got himself a cute little lady to while away his time."

"What the hell you talking about?" Finn LeFort, and beside him, Ollie, stared incredulously at this piece of information.

Gans was so impatient he was cracking his knuckles. "What old man and what girl? God damn it, tell it or shut up! One!"

"Preacher man. A real bible pounder. And a girl." Box wet his lips vigorously. "Young. He could be her paw. We never got that close to find out. But we seen 'em, me and Dutch. And that girl, she is the cutest-looking piece of goods a man could lay his eyes on this good while, let me tell you. And she is giving it all to Slocum. Slocum is getting it right up to as far as he can shove it!"

"Well, by God!" The words broke from Gans, and a long silence followed.

"You telling the straight of it, you two weasels?" Porky stood hard in front of them.

"That is the honest-to-God's truth!"

Porky had his hand on the butt of his sixgun, though

he had not drawn it. "You lie on this and I'll pistol whip the both of you to your elbows and knees, you sons of bitches!"

"Porky, it's the truth!"

The two of them stared in dismay at the LeForts, thoroughly thrown by the turn their news had taken. They had expected triumph, forgiveness, maybe even a reward, a celebration.

Gans's voice was dangerously soft. "An' what else?"

Wagner wet his lips with the tip of his tongue. "That wagon is riding far back. They got real privacy, like."

"And Slocum. How do you know he's been getting it?"

"Seen him and her coming out of the bushes. Shit, you can tell."

"Broke our ass gettin' back here to tell you," Dillman put in. "You could give us a drink."

"Well, by God! I'll be whang-danged!" And Big Gans let out a hoot and a holler that was close to ear-splitting.

"How d'you like that?" chuckled Print, his eyes disappearing in tears of laughter. "Maybe that little lady's what can soften up the son of a bitch."

Gans was suddenly scowling.

"That bastard is always gettin' it! Maybe you're right, Print, boy. Maybe that will be what plays him our way." He turned his head toward Wagner and Dillman, his big eyes boring in. "That wagon is still with them?"

"It was there when we left."

"At the Little Wichita?"

"Close. Two, three miles south."

Dillman and Wagner were both clearly showing

their relief at finally having made a score when suddenly, without any warning, Gans LeFort's huge hand closed on Dutch Dillman's sore arm. Gans's grip was like a bear trap clamping his elbow. The pain stabbed through Dillman's entire body.

"You got one more chance to prove you might be allowed to ride with some part of this outfit. I say *some* part. Not the whole of it. Not the senior boys. You understand?"

Dillman nodded, biting his lip to handle the pain.

"You two kids bust yer asses back there to the Little Wichita and hold yer eye on things till you hear from me."

"Sure, Gans."

"If you run into them Arap scouts, I want to see them."

"Sure."

"Meanwhile, don't do nothing. Just hold yer eye there. I will be letting you know what to do."

They nodded, relieved to be gone. And as they rode out of earshot Dutch turned to his companion. "The sons of bitches didn't even offer us a drink."

"Nothing to eat neither," snapped Box.

They rode in silence side by side, and after a while Dutch said, "Box, you thinking what I'm thinking?"

Box was grinning. "I sure am."

"And I'm thinking something else, too, besides the girl," Dutch said after another moment.

"Yeah? What?"

"Slocum. We're going to get that son of a bitch." He held out his injured arm. "And fuck the LeForts!"

"Both at one time, huh?" Box's grin was all over his face.

"Both at one time, Box."

"Slocum and the girl."

"And fuck the LeForts!"

They rode chuckling down the trail.

"The river is still high," Slocum said as he cantered the roan horse up to where young Denny was watching the herd. "But she's coming down."

He had just spoken those words when Little Coyote's men hit the west side of the herd, whooping and screaming, popping blankets and firing their rifles, using no halters but guiding their ponies with their knees as they raced up and down, terrifying the cattle.

By the time Slocum and the cowboys reached that side of the herd, the Indians were gone. But the jittery cattle were starting to run. And now a second bunch of shrieking marauders hit them from the east. And again they were gone, whooping down the long slope toward the swollen river.

"Hold them!" Slocum shouted. "Let the riders go, but hold the cows!"

Dinwiddie came pounding up on a big steel-dust gray gelding. The cattleman didn't waste his breath cursing, but began working his horse in toward the charging cattle, trying to turn them.

"Drive them to the river!" shouted Slocum. "They won't cross, and we can bunch them there!"

But there was no holding them. The cattle broke and ran. Hours later, the men were still rounding up the shattered herd.

Dinwiddie was furious. "I'm getting goddamn sick of this shit, let me tell you!"

"That is just what the LeForts are up to," Slocum said calmly, lighting a quirly. "They want us shook and mad and played out by the time we get up north; and we'll be sitting pretty for them."

"What I mean is, I'd sure like to get my hands on those boys!"

"We will." Slocum had stepped down from his horse. "We'll camp. I believe maybe tomorrow we'll be able to cross. She's starting to go down now, and we can try that place down there by those willows."

Slocum instructed the men now to work in threes, and to take no unnecessary chances. "Two of you'll be working the cows, and the third will be the lookout, with his guns ready."

"It is a long way to Kansas, even if we are up in Arapaho country," Dinwiddie said wearily as he sat down for evening grub. His anger had cooled. He squinted at the sun, which was blazing at the horizon just before going down. "Reckon Nellie's seeing to her chores right now." And he grinned sheepishly at Slocum.

"You horny old man."

"I ain't all that old, young feller."

"Well, you'll be seeing her soon."

"That's what I know. By God," and he lowered his voice. "I am looking forward to her biscuits." And he made a terrible face, nodding in the direction of Heavy Pete, who was standing outside his chuck wagon. His eyes hung on Slocum. "The men are tired."

"Are you?"

"I don't have time," he said, taking a pull at his coffee. "You say we can cross them tomorrer?"

"Maybe. Late afternoon, or the next morning, for sure." Slocum got to his feet. "I'll be paying a friendly visit to Yellow Eagle."

"The chief?"

He nodded. "We need friendly relations with him."

"Are you going to tell him about those goddamn

stampeders? Make him get them off us. Ain't they from his tribe?"

"I am sure Yellow Eagle disowned them long ago."

"So how do you figure he's going to help us?"

Slocum spat, his eyes sweeping the dusky prairie. "We need scouts. We need to keep scouts out all the time now we're getting close."

"You know Yellow Eagle? Is he a friendly?"

"He was one of their great warriors. Now he's a peace chief, but not a paper chief." Slocum thought a minute and then he said, "I dunno. I guess, like some others, he's seen that you can't beat what's going to happen anyway."

The Indian encampment on Punished Woman Creek was quiet as Slocum rode in, the grass whispering against his horse's feet. There was no sign of any human or animal. Still, he knew he was being watched, and had been for some time. He rode in openly, boldly, but in a friendly way.

It was cool now, entering the grove of cottonwood trees, with the shadows deeper and mingling with each other. A thrush sang its song, and overhead, through the cathedral of trees, he watched an eagle soar. From the Indian pony herd came the tinkle of a grazing bell. A dog barked, and at once others joined in. Now the smell of the cookfires mixed with the odor of the trees and the good sweat smell of his horse.

Breaking into a clearing, he came upon a group of young boys playing the hoop game. Farther on, some older boys were playing buffalo hunt. But now, seeing the white man riding in, they stopped and stood staring with no expression on their faces.

He smelled the cookfires stronger now. More dogs were barking, and though he didn't turn his head to look, he was aware of the women standing near their lodges looking at him in total silence.

Suddenly three warriors appeared on horseback. He had been expecting them, had been surprised that he'd been allowed this far into the camp without confrontation.

Raising his right hand in the gesture of peace, he drew rein. The approaching warriors carried feathered lances; each wore a single feather in his scalp lock. They halted their ponies about six yards from Slocum.

"I come asking for talk with Chief Yellow Eagle," Slocum said, signing it with his hands. "I am Slocum. I am friend of the Arapaho. Once, many snows past, in the Moon of the Dark Red Calves, I spoke with Yellow Eagle on the Washita. I hope the chief will remember his friend Slocum." He paused, watching them carefully. When they didn't respond, he went on. "Down there..." He pointed. "I bring herd of many cows. Many beeves go north. I come to Yellow Eagle to ask his help."

The three remained silent, still watching him. He knew they were reading every detail of his face, his body, the way he sat the buckskin horse, his very breathing. Nothing seemed beyond their scrutiny. And Slocum knew that mostly they were feeling him out.

It was the middle warrior of the three who finally spoke. He was a lean, copper-colored young man, with his mouth set in a straight line. "You come from the many cows," he said, speaking Catholic Mission English. "I am Water Singing. Yellow Eagle waits for you." His words came slowly and clearly, and he didn't use his hands at all.

Turning their horses, they escorted him further into the camp. More lodges appeared through the trees, and the odors of the cookfires intensified as he watched the steam rising from the big black kettles.

In his lodge, Yellow Eagle was sitting with three of his headmen in the customary circle when Water Singing entered with Slocum. Slocum was well aware of tipi ritual, and he waited while the chief indicated a place at his right.

The Arapaho was a stocky man with no unnecessary weight on his firm, well-proportioned body. A man of more than sixty winters, Slocum knew, though it was difficult to tell an Indian's age according to white standards. For a long moment they sat in silence and Slocum began to feel the tremendous energy coming from Yellow Eagle's serene stillness.

In quiet dignity the chief waited. Slocum knew he was waiting for the moment when everything needed for the meeting would be there. And finally, when Yellow Eagle was satisfied that it was so, that those present were sufficiently relaxed and attentive and the words spoken could be truer, he drew the pipe from its special fur-lined pouch.

The preparation, followed by the offering of the pipe, was done in full silence, with absolute attention. As Slocum watched, he remembered other times he had witnessed the simple ceremony. Each movement, he knew, had to be performed in a certain way, for it had a special meaning, and so nothing in the ritual must be changed.

It had always pleased him to watch the way certain of the older Indians moved. Even the simplest gestures seemed somehow more pure, containing a supple strength and precision which the younger men had not yet learned. He had noticed how, even when moving quickly, Yellow Eagle seemed to be aware of something; something else. As though listening.

When the pipe had been offered and sent around the circle in the prescribed manner, the chief spoke in halting English.

"Now we can speak together, for we have smoked; and because we have smoked together, what is said will be true." And he turned his eyes on Slocum.

"I have come to ask your help, Yellow Eagle," Slocum began, wondering if the chief remembered him.

"My scouts have told me of your cows, Slow-Come. The ones with the long horns on their heads. They are many. And I have been told of the water rising, and Little Coyote's band making the cows runaway." He picked up the eagle-wing fan that was lying on the blanket beside him and started to fan himself.

"I see that Little Coyote was not sent by you, but he is working with the gray men who are trying to keep the cows from going north to Kansas," Slocum said. "Can you stop Little Coyote from chasing the cows?"

"Little Coyote has been told that he must not do these things; but, like others of the young men, he and his friends are not happy. They have not had the warrior days behind them, like myself and the older warriors, and so they long to hunt, to fight, to count coup."

He turned toward his three headmen and spoke in Arapaho. When he was through the three old men muttered, *"Hou! Hou!"*

"I understand how it is, Yellow Eagle. It is hard to no longer have the freedom to come and go as one wishes." Slocum looked at the three headmen. "I understand it well."

"You see, it is their heritage to be warriors," the

chief said. "But the gray men have come and they give them whiskey and then make them do bad things. Last time they did that I ordered them pony-whipped. This time—I have spoken to my headmen, and it is agreed that Little Coyote and his men will be banished unless they come in to council before ten sleeps have passed."

A long silence fell, while Slocum felt the weight of the chief's words and the sorrow and anger that were in them.

One of the headmen now spoke, but using his hands as well, for the words were halting, and not sure as to meaning, and so the signing supported what was meant to be said. It was the Indian immediately to Yellow Eagle's left.

"The young men are restless in this time of the rising again of the earth. In former times we would have a buffalo hunt, or we would fight with the Crows or Shoshone. But now we must all stay in this place and not go some place where we would wish to go. The young men especially do not want to be hang-around-the-forts. They want to be men."

"But to be a man one must follow the way of the warrior," Yellow Eagle said, coming in quickly. "A warrior does not always do what he likes to do. And the trouble is, Little Coyote can bring anger between the Arapaho and the whites. And it is because of the whiskey. No! Little Coyote must come in to council."

And the headmen, including the one who had spoken, all nodded in agreement, saying, *"Hou! Hou!"*

Yellow Eagle turned toward Slocum. "But you see, Slow-Come. If we Indians go to the gray men and stop their whiskey, then the whites will say we are making war on them. Then the pony soldiers will come and put us in the iron house and maybe kill us. No—we can do nothing."

"Yellow Eagle. I have come to ask you for scouts to help me with the cows. I hear what you have said about Little Coyote. Will you send me scouts to help me, and I will try to stop the gray men with the whiskey-giving? I know they have given the whiskey and guns, too, to the Comanche and Kiowa, because they wish not to allow any cows to go north."

"Why is that?" one of the headmen who had not yet spoken asked.

"It is because they want the cows to come to another place, where they can sell them."

"I am afraid that when more of the whiskey is given others of our people will take it and then there may be a big trouble with the whites and the soldier men." Yellow Eagle put down his fan. "I will send you scouts. We will help each other. We have already spoken of it in council."

And, reaching forward, he lifted the pipe and, closing his eyes slightly, gestured with it in a certain way.

"We will smoke," he said.

It was late in the day when Slocum left Yellow Eagle standing outside his lodge. For a moment they stood together saying nothing as the sun slipped down behind the cottonwoods and box elders. The smells of the cooking of the evening meal were very strong.

Slocum had brought tobacco as a gift and had given it at the time he entered the tipi, but now he said, "Will you send some men besides the four scouts, to whom I can give meat for your cookfires?"

The Indian stood next to him in his fringed buckskin shirt with the little bells on it that tinkled when he moved. The wind blew softly in the camp clearing and Slocum watched the shadows thrown by the buckskin fringes as the chief raised his arm and pointed toward the setting sun.

"They will come before the sun is there again," he said.

As Slocum rode away, he could feel the chief's eyes on him for a long time.

Slocum was suddenly awake. Lying on his bedroll with not a muscle moving, yet breathing easily, he listened; listened with the precision that had guided him all these years on the trail, in the saloons, in the cribs and fancy houses, at the gaming tables, on the riverboats, in Frisco and in Denver, in Jicarilla and End-of-Track—through all the action that made up a full life. Though still a young man, John Slocum shared with the true old timers the knowledge that he was one of a dying breed. It gave him a bittersweet joy and a big freedom.

As always he had slept fully clothed with his hand on his Colt, and now he rose swiftly to a crouch, not missing a sound in the sighing of the early dawn. Straightening to his full height, he slid the Colt into its holster, which was still buckled around his waist.

He waited, again letting himself receive the full impression of the sleeping camp. Nothing out of the ordinary. One of the picket horses nickered, and a couple of longhorns got to their feet clumsily and took a few steps and lay down again. Across the clearing Otis Dinwiddie's wet snores broke unevenly into the dry morning.

He had placed the men with care, setting the times for relief of duties, making it firm, like in the army, for all of them knew that there wasn't much time now.

He had sent Yellow Eagle's scouts ahead to find

the LeForts. From now on he was going to need steady information as to their moves.

And now, once again, looking at the sky, he saw that his inner sense of time had not failed him. He had awakened just as he had planned. Like an animal; some said like an Indian. His raven-black hair pointed to Indian blood in his veins. Cherokee, some thought; others said just plain poison.

The moon was not yet down, while the sky was lightening fast. He didn't hurry. He drew the headstall over the buckskin, worked the bit into its mouth, then saddled him. Buck liked to swell his belly at such times when he was feeling zippy, so that the unwary rider putting his foot in the stirrup would find a loose cinch had dumped him with his saddle hanging upside down on Buck's belly.

"Stop that," Slocum muttered, and smacked him in the ribs. Buck didn't mind. He turned his head back fast and tried for a bite on Slocum's arm as the cinch tightened. This time, Slocum smacked him on the nose. Both of them felt better as the man stepped into the saddle.

As a rule he rode in a wide circle around the cattle, and this morning he started on the other side of the river, far ahead of the herd.

He had seen no sign of Little Coyote's band since the last stampede. A soft wind stirred through the land now, and as the light grew stronger behind the eastern horizon, earth and sky seemed to melt into each other. He rode close to the trees along the river and on raised ground wherever he could, keening to every nuance of sound and smell.

They would bring the herd over the river this day, he decided, for the water had gone down considerably. They'd lost too damn much time already. He was sitting his horse just at the edge of the box elders, studying the terrain for a likely spot to drive the animals across, when he heard behind him the loud click of a revolver hammer being drawn back, and the voice, which was more an insistent whisper.

"Slocum!"

He was already out of the saddle as the sixgun cracked out the shot and the buckskin horse screamed as the bullet nicked his rump.

Slocum landed close to a thick bush, coming up fast with the big Colt in his fist. In the instant that his eye caught the flicker of movement to his right he fired; the cry of pain telling him he'd scored. Immediately the crack of a second gun sounded to his left, and he felt the bullet creasing the top of his left shoulder. He pumped three rounds instantly, and there was no return. In the next moment he heard two horses galloping away.

He did not give pursuit, aware that it could be a trap, with a third bushwhacker waiting for him to show himself. Instead he waited, and only when satisfied that there had only been the two guns did he start looking for tracks.

It was easy enough to find where the two men had stood, separately, waiting to catch him in crossfire. They were wearing trail boots and riding shod horses. He saw no signs of blood, but figured he had wounded the one, though probably not badly. Then he saw the piece of blue cloth. It was a bandanna. Lots of trail men wore blue bandannas, but the only one he'd noticed lately with a big tear in it was the bandanna Dutch Dillman had wrapped his arm in after Slocum had pistol-whipped it.

He caught the buckskin and gentled him, and mounted carefully, for the animal was still spooked.

By God, he was thinking, the LeForts were getting down to it now. And why not? They had the time and the men and they could pick off the KC men one by one. Including himself.

Except, he reflected ruefully, they'd better put together some better shooting than that pair of greenhorn kids.

As he was riding back to the campsite, his shoulder began to hurt and he remembered he'd been shot. But he couldn't find much blood.

"The son of a bitch elevated a little too high," Dinwiddie observed when he'd had a look. "You think it was them two kids with the itchy feelings and fingers?"

"I'll bet on it."

"Think they're with the LeForts?"

"More than likely."

"They'll be back. They're bent on counting coup."

"I expect 'em."

"You were lucky," Dinwiddie observed.

"No," Slocum said. "They were."

8

All day the yellow plain had shimmered in the heat. Even now in the late afternoon, with the men trying to throw them on the bed ground, the steers were staggering and haggard. Nor were the men in any better condition. Slocum had ordered a dry camp with all hands ready for instant action. The four Arapaho scouts sent by Yellow Eagle reported no sign of water ahead; all the water holes and creeks were dried up.

"First we catch more water'n we can handle, and now we don't get enough to wash a tooth!" Dinwiddie spat a dry clot of chewing tobacco in the direction of a jackrabbit who suddenly found the energy to bound away out of range. "What you find for tomorrer?" he asked Slocum, who had just come riding up to the chuck wagon.

Slocum, his eyes red-rimmed, his lungs dusty from his daily scout ahead for the next day's drive, swung down from his horse, grounding the reins. "More of the same," he said, eyeing the gaunt cattleman. "All I can tell you is we're getting closer."

"Scouts find anything different?"

"It's dry as a bone all the way to the Canadian." He had been riding the spotted horse, and now he slipped the bridle out of the animal's mouth and let the head stall lie back on his neck so he could more freely crop the bunch grass that was so dry it seemed to crackle. Then he loosened the horse's cinch and patted him on his sweating flank.

"The Arapahoes tell me the LeForts are coming in north of the Canadian," he said.

"How far?"

"Close enough to hit us when we cross the water."

"Shit." Dinwiddie started to spit, but found his mouth was too dry. "By the time we get to the Canadian we'll be plumb dried out and the animals will be gaunted all to hell." He let his eyes wander over the water-starved ground with its gaping cracks and treacherous footing for the haggard, restive cattle. "We'll be a cinch for the LeForts." He ran the palm of his hand hard along his game hip and said, "'Least we got us four good men from Yellow Eagle, then."

"We could use more."

"You fixing to ask him for more?"

"He wants to stop the whiskey. I'm thinking when we settle the LeForts we can also get shut of the whiskey. Yellow Eagle could see it that way."

Dinwiddie sniffed. He took out his plug of tobacco to peel a chew, looked at it wryly, and put it back in his pocket. "Soon enough, a man won't have enough juice left in him to spit!" He watched Slocum lighting a quirly.

"Well, Dinwiddie, at least you can't claim the critters ain't road-broke by now."

This brought a smile to the cattleman's eyes. "We got some water from the creek there," he said. "About enough for the horses if we take it easy, and for the chuck wagon. But the critters..." He let the rest of his sentence hang as he swung down from the claybank gelding and walked with Slocum toward the chuck wagon, and a beleaguered Heavy Pete O'Hay.

"Ain't gonna make it without water," Pete said.

"We're going to make it." Slocum reached for the coffee pot. "Maybe we'll have to boil the coffee with cow piss, and maybe that'll give it an interesting flavor," he went on, his remark bringing wry expressions to the faces of his two companions.

With coffee in him, Dinwiddie suddenly said, "The men are real tired, Slocum."

"You're saying that you are."

The cattleman straightened, rubbing his hip and nodding a little. He took a pull at his coffee. "You catch a man right fast, Slocum," he said. "I appreciate that." And he grinned. "Tell you one thing; if my little woman was standing right there I wouldn't be tired. I'd have her down right now!"

And they both chuckled at that, while Slocum's thoughts turned to Ava Muldoon.

He felt Otis Dinwiddie's eyes on him. "I do believe that Reverend feller was carrying something. He had that look about him. But I liked the both of them."

"You think those were summer names?" Slocum asked.

"I wouldn't say no."

"I had the same thought." Slocum shrugged. "But this country is full of people with summer names." He turned back toward his horse, who was cropping the grass nearby. "I like it that way."

"Won't do you any good if you didn't," Dinwiddie said, drolly canting his head.

It was nightfall now, and still the thirsty cattle wouldn't settle. All night long they milled, and by dawn the men were more exhausted than they'd ever thought they could be.

"We're driving straight to the Canadian," Slocum told them. "I mean I want them pushed. It isn't all that far."

There was grumbling, but they read the sense in it. And he saw that.

"Those cows will appreciate that water," said Heavy Pete. "Those that make it."

"They're all gonna make it; even if we have to hogtie 'em and carry them horseback," Slocum told him.

But he didn't say to anyone what was really on his mind, though he was pretty sure Dinwiddie must have thought of it. It was going to be next to impossible to hold the herd once they got a smell of the water at the Canadian River. It would take every man to keep them from bolting. And it would be the perfect moment for the LeForts to attack.

It was the next morning when he had roped out the tough little buckskin and was saddling him that he heard the horse's hooves booming on the hard ground like a drum. Bear Sings, one of Yellow Eagle's scouts, was quirting his brown and white pony on both flanks, drubbing the animal's ribs with moccasined heels as he raced in to where the horse wrangler had put up the rope corral. He pulled up tight in a small cloud of dust a short distance from Slocum, jumped down from the pony, and with the hackamore still in his hand, walked forward.

Slocum took note of the Arapaho not coming so close that the plume of dust raised by his pulling to such a tight halt enveloped himself. Yellow Eagle had his men well trained.

Bear Sings was a short, stocky young man with a pleasing disposition and a good sense of humor. Right now he was grave and excited at the same time, as he signed with his hands.

"Wagon!" And he pointed down the herd's back trail.

"How far?" signed Slocum.

Bear Sings indicated a good distance, pointing to the sun, then indicating with his hand how far it would move by the time someone rode back to the wagon.

"How many wagons?"

The Arapaho held up one finger.

"Horses?"

Bear Sings signed that there was a team of big blaze-faced bays pulling the wagon, plus a black gelding saddle horse with three white stockings tied to the endgate.

"Did you see the people?"

The Indian shook his head.

"Where is Kicking Horse?"

Bear Sings signed that Kicking Horse was up ahead looking for water, while Quick Walker and Tail were scouting the flanks of the herd.

Slocum asked if Bear Sings had scouted the area around the wagon, but the Arapaho said no, signing that he had come back quickly to tell Slocum the news. Then he asked whether the team was hitched, and the scout said that all three horses had been stripped; the black gelding still tied to the endgate, the team tied to two wagon wheels. He added that the wagon was on the shadowed side of a timber-fringed gulch.

Slocum swung onto the buckskin. He supposed it was all right. They had evidently camped the night before and were not yet up and about when Bear Sings had seen the wagon.

Still, there was something bothering him, and he couldn't pin it. Bear Sings waited while his pony shook his head and kicked at the deer flies, which were numerous.

And then he had it. "Bear Sings, I go to the wagon," he said, moving his hands in the sign language. "You follow on my back trail. But not too close."

The young Arapaho leaped onto his pony and sat there straight as an arrow, his bronze skin gleaming in the sunlight. He was grinning.

"Good enough," Slocum muttered to himself. Good enough. For a man didn't grow old out in this country through being simple-minded and careless.

Of course, he had known right along it wouldn't work. Something in her voice, her manner—and in the Reverend's, too—had shouted to him that no, they were not going to do what he'd told them. Something in him had known they would be back. Yet, they were evidently not intending to catch up, but to follow along. Maybe they'd try to catch up if they got frightened or felt the need for protection. But judging from the way they'd camped, stripping the horses, they were in no hurry to catch up with the herd. He wondered how long they'd been following. Probably they never did make it to Medicine Bluff. And he found himself smiling at her deception.

Crazy, he told himself. They were crazy. She was plumb crazy. But that didn't settle anything. The West was full of crazy people. Full of people who would not take no for an answer.

It was right on noon when he came to the timber that ran along the edge of the narrow gulch. The wagon was just as Bear Sings had described, stopped near the trees, but no longer in shadow. The horses were standing in the broiling sun. No one had bothered to move them.

As Slocum rode the buckskin along the edge of the timber toward the wagon and horses, the black saddle horse raised his head to look at them and nickered.

Slocum had in the same instant reached forward to put his hand across Buck's nostrils so he wouldn't answer and give them away.

Now he drew rein and studied the small clearing. There was no sign of life coming from the wagon; no evidence outside that they had built a cookfire. Everything had the mark of desertion on it.

Had no one seen him? Hadn't they heard that horse nicker, and been warned that someone might be approaching?

Or... He was being over-cautious. Likely they were inside the wagon talking or praying or something, oblivious to what might be happening outside in the world. Innocence, he reflected. There was indeed something wildly innocent about her. He had surely seen that when they had made love. And suddenly the thought of seeing her again, touching her and being touched, brought desire pounding in his body. But he drove the thought away, knowing it was no time for indulgence. Men lost their lives when they indulged themselves.

He kicked the buckskin forward now, loosening the hammer thong on his Colt at the same time. When he was a few feet from the wagon, he halted and called out.

"Hello! Hello inside the wagon!"

There was no answer.

He didn't call again, but sat his horse, letting his eyes move slowly around the fringe of timber that lined the little gulch.

Presently he stepped down from the buckskin, and with his Colt in his right hand, with his other he reached up and pulled the Henry out of its scabbard. Up close to the wagon now, he called again. There was still no answer.

Cautiously, he dropped the Colt into its holster, took the Henry in his right hand with his finger on the trigger, and with his left gripped the arm rest on the wagon seat, stepped onto one of the front wheel spokes, and swung up.

Switching hands with the Henry and drawing the Colt again, he ducked under the canvas flap and was inside the wagon.

They were lying on the floor, both bound and gagged. The girl was struggling to get loose. The Reverend Muldoon was motionless.

It took him only a moment to cut them free. He helped Ava to her feet and for a moment she clung to him, then dropped down beside her uncle, who was beginning to move slowly.

"Oh, my God," she murmured. "Are you all right?"

"Yes, my dear. I am all right," he said as she helped him sit up. He was shaking all over, blinking his eyes, wincing.

"Who did it?" Slocum asked, looking at the dark bruise on the girl's face.

"Two men. They came when we were asleep. The first thing I knew there was a gun in my face."

But she was more concerned with her uncle than with herself. It took a while to revive him fully; he'd been beaten. Water and then straight whiskey helped alleviate some of his pain.

"They came at night." Muldoon's chest was heaving, the pain filling his face as he told of the two men who had appeared out of nowhere. He fell silent then, staring into a corner of the wagon.

"And then what?" Slocum asked.

The Reverend Muldoon's lips quivered. He clenched his fists. "I—I want to kill them! God damn them!" It was his anger that brought back his strength.

"What did they do?" Slocum asked, turning to Ava. But seeing again the big dark blue lump on her face, her cut mouth and torn clothing, he already knew.

"God almighty..." he muttered.

The girl was looking at her uncle. "Miller, you mustn't...It was all right. It wasn't...It was all right. It will be all right, my dear..." And she kissed his cheek, stroked his head with both her hands.

She sat now with her arm around him, his head lying on her breast. For a while they just stayed like that while she comforted him. Finally his rage subsided and he began trying to comfort her. For a moment Slocum saw them as two small, hurt children.

"I'm all right now," Muldoon said.

Slocum suddenly realized that Ava was looking at him.

"You're wondering," she said.

"It's not my business."

"Yes, it is, John." There were tears standing in her eyes, but they didn't fall. "He's my husband."

"Yes, I see."

"No, you can't, really." She still had her arms around Muldoon, while he clung to her hand. "Please, let's talk," she went on, her eyes begging him. "But later...there is more..."

Slocum nodded.

He sat absolutely still now, listening, putting it all together while she watched him.

"Do you think they're outside?" she asked, and he caught the alarm in her voice.

"I don't know. How long ago were they here?"

"I don't know. Oh, I don't know."

It was then that they heard the drumming of a horse's hooves and a guttural voice calling.

"My God, it's the Indians!"

"Only one," Slocum said easily, getting up and going through the canvas flap. "Come on out, both of you."

The sunlight slanting across the tops of the timber into the gulch caught the bronze sheen of Bear Sings's near-naked body as he sat his brown and white pony.

There was something heavy lying across his horse's withers, and now, with a grunt, the scout pushed the dead man off so that he fell to the ground. The pony, relieved of the weight, took two little steps forward and, raising his long ears, looked off into the distance.

Bear Sings dropped to the ground and turned the body over. It was Box Wagner.

"He wait kill you when you come out of wagon. Good you tell me follow back trail."

Box Wagner looked even younger than when he was alive, Slocum thought. He was reminded of the pieces dolls that some of the Sioux children made out of materials just lying around. Box Wagner looked like a pieces doll as he lay crumpled and small in the bright green grass.

"Second man get away," Bear Sings said. "You want me follow?" He spoke carefully, yet with enthusiasm, and not using his hands at all. He had counted coup.

"Let him go. We'll catch up with him sooner or later."

"Second man get away fast. He see me smell him. Smell his tracks. He give many tracks to Bear Sings's smell." And he broke into laughter.

"I didn't know you spoke English," Slocum said. "How come?"

Bear Sings was a young man who took delight in

many things. His grin spread all over his face. And he almost giggled as he said, "How come? Slow-Come?"

9

For two days the cattle had no water. Heavy Pete had managed to find a small amount for the horses. The men were rationing theirs. They were irritable and exhausted, but Slocum had them up at dawn pushing the herd as hard as possible. Many of the weaker steers were starting to cave in. It was so bad the horses' bits had to be steeped in water before the bridles were put on, or the animals' mouths would blister.

And then—out of nowhere it seemed—came the rain.

"Praise the Lord." Dinwiddie lifted his scarlet-rimmed eyes to the skies, letting the rain wash over him.

The cattle milled, honking and bellowing with excitement as the smell of the water overpowered them. It came down harder, soon filling the buffalo wallows and the nearby creek. It rained all night and into the following day. The herd kept milling, but it didn't stampede. The men held on to them grimly. Slocum kept three shifts of night guards posted over the animals. The men began rubbing tobacco juice into their eyes to keep awake.

In the afternoon the rain stopped and Slocum ordered the herd moved a few miles west, and grazed them until dark. They were bedded in a strip of low hills. The next day's drive put them in an area where rain had been plentiful and where there was good grass and a lot of water.

There was still no sign of the LeForts or of Little Coyote's band. The Arapaho scouts reported the LeForts camped on the north side of the Canadian River near Carpenters Pass. They had a number of outriders on the watch, and it was not possible for either Bear Sings or Kicking Horse to get in close. All they could tell Slocum was that there were a lot of men at the pass.

The girl and Muldoon had remained much to themselves since rejoining the cattle drive. Slocum had respected their wish for privacy, exchanging only a few words in passing. He had no time for more, in any case. He knew she wanted to talk to him, but he would let it come from her. Meanwhile, he kept his eye on her to see how she was mending.

It happened the evening before the final push to the Canadian. He was giving his spotted horse a brushdown with a handful of leafless little twigs which he'd broken off for the purpose.

He had his back to her as she approached, yet he knew she was there.

"Can I talk to you?"

He turned to look at her. Even though her face was drawn, and he knew she couldn't have been sleeping well, she carried herself with the quiet dignity he found so appealing. Her spirit was still as strong as ever in her.

"I don't want to interrupt your work," she said.

"I'm done." He tossed the handful of twigs onto a clump of sagebrush.

"Pete says we'll be crossing the river soon and there'll be a big fight."

"That's what it's getting to look like."

They had quite easily fallen into step and were strolling toward the edge of the campsite. The sun was just down and there was that moment of blending of day and night, with each carrying the other as they both separated and yet were still somehow united.

"I want to thank you for taking us back," she said, her voice soft. "I really see that you were right in sending us away. I...I won't ask you to forgive me." And he felt rather than actually saw her small smile as she turned her face full view toward him. Yet he realized she was deadly serious.

"Do you understand what I meant about there being no forgiveness out here?" he asked.

She nodded. "Yes, I think so. I've thought about that a lot. That's why I just said it."

He kicked a piece of loose sage out of their path, but without breaking the rhythm of their walking. "How's your...husband?"

She stopped now and faced him. They were close to the horse remuda and there was no one about. He was looking at one of her ears, which turned in slightly at the top. Because of the rain and then the heat she had pulled her hair back. He had a tremendous urge to kiss her on her ear. At the same time, his erection was making him quite uncomfortable and he had to shift his stance.

"Miller is all right. Depressed, though. They beat him, you know. Those men."

She raised her head to look directly at him and he saw that the swelling on her cheekbone had gone down somewhat, though it was still discolored. Without thinking, he reached out and touched it with his fingers. She didn't take his hand away, but he felt the tears on his fingers.

"I'm sorry." She took his hand and held it, and with her other hand wiped her eyes. "Self-pity is disgusting, isn't it?"

"Sometimes it can help."

She let go of his hand. "I won't tell you a long story," she said in a new, firmer voice. "My mother died when I was very young. I never met my father. I was an orphan. I ran away. I had no money. Nothing. Miller helped me. I met him when I was only fifteen. He was kind. He treated me in a decent way, respected me. Even then the men were attracted to me. It started when I was very young. But Miller, he wasn't like the others. He treated me... well, he was a good man. A very good man."

"I understand."

"I know you do. That's why I can tell you."

"So you married him," Slocum said.

She nodded. "I was happy. But then sometimes not so happy."

"I can understand that, too."

"And... Miller understood it." She took a little step back from him and looked quickly around her, as though she'd forgotten where she was. "Those men. The two. Somehow they knew about us, John. They saw us somehow, walking together, probably. And guessed something." She shook her head, finished with that part of what she wanted to say.

"Anyhow, they taunted Miller about it, tried to humiliate him. Oh, he's not a preacher. You've guessed that, I'm sure. He's a gambler. He bought that organ and the hymn books from the widow of a parson who was on the wagon train. The parson died about a week after we left St. Joseph. Miller thought the preacher story would make a good cover for him." She smiled suddenly. "He's not exactly an Honest John. But, for God's sake, don't breathe it. I'm just trying to tell you."

"Is that why you left the other wagon train?"

"Somebody accused him of cheating. And it was a gentleman who carried a couple of guns. We were invited to leave. Or at least Miller was. I was asked to stay."

"So they were also after you, the men."

"Oh, yes. And so we left." She suddenly released a quick little sigh. "And then you found us."

"I wish you could leave this one," Slocum said. "But it's too late now. The army is very far away, so there's no place to send you. I doubt you'd make it anyway."

"We'll be fine. The only thing that worries me is, I don't want either of us to be in the way. We want to help. Miller is eager to help. He knows how to shoot a gun."

"We can use him. And you, too," he added.

"He's been showing me how to shoot."

The sky was still more with the day than the night and so there was enough light to see clearly, even though the sun had disappeared behind the rim of the far hills. He had slipped his arm around her shoulders and she leaned lightly against him. Gently he reached over and turned her face toward him. Her lips, still bruised, were warm and sweet on his, and for a moment her body seemed to melt. But only for a moment. Then it was as though something organic in her remembered, and she tightened.

"I want you," she said. "But I can't now."

"It's not the moment. There's plenty of time." He kissed her ear. "I never realized what wonderful ears you had."

"There's more to me than my ears."

"I happen to know." He grinned down at her. And

then he was serious. "How bad did they hurt you?"

She looked up at him and then stepped back a little. "They tried to rape me."

"Tried?"

"I kicked one of them right where he won't ever forget it."

"Good for you. And the other?"

"I suppose he did it. I don't know. That bruise on my face isn't the only one. I've got a few all over." She looked down at her hands, which she was holding together at her waist. "It could have been a lot worse." Her eyes returned to his. "I want you—but in a while. Is that all right?"

Slocum didn't say anything. He took her hand and opened it in his, and then, lifting it, he bent his head and touched his lips to her palm.

In the cool, soft evening Miller Muldoon flicked through the new deck of cards he had just opened. It bothered him that his hands and his fingers were stiff. He was definitely out of practice, a condition he had never allowed during his many years of assiduous application to his craft. But the two men, Dillman and Wagner, had twisted his arms during the course of beating him, and one of them had slammed a gun barrel across the knuckles of his right hand.

Certainly such things were not to be unexpected in the course of his profession, but as a result he was right now far from the sleek second dealer from top, bottom, or middle of a deck, the nimble reader of marked cards, unsurpassed at outgaming opponents, a man to be feared across the baize-topped tables of more than a few cowtowns and even in certain areas of Frisco, St. Louis, Denver, and Fort Worth. Miller Muldoon's reputation was that of a man who could slicker a preacher right out of his Sunday morning take quicker than a cat could yawn. And Miller Muldoon was enjoying the role of reverend, as in the past he had favored that of doctor, drummer, circus impresario, not to mention saloonkeeper and purveyor of various and sundry tonics, syrups, pills, ointments, liniments, and all manner of profitable nostrums, as well as a short but thriving career in transporting prospective wives from the eastern areas of civilization out to the frontier where the demand for them was heavy. Withal, he had never ceased to practice his art and craft, honing his unique talents with his holdouts, shiners, trimmers, marked cards, shaved dice, and other advantageous tools of the trade, not to mention the blue-tinted spectacles which enabled the wearer to detect marks made on the backs of cards with phosphorescent ink, which was invisible to the unaided eyes of an opponent, or the various rings, pins, cuffs, hidden pockets, all contributing to the good fortune and longevity of the one and only Miller Muldoon.

Not much higher than the white stockings on a cow pony, Miller had gone to school in the great tradition, as apprentice to a master who plied the riverboats of the Mississippi, but also worked the railroads and stages and hotels of the West.

"Colonel" Beau DeWallace literally lavished his copious knowledge on the young boy. When in his cups, and only then, he claimed to be the lad's father. Young Miller accepted the drama of their two roles and lived a happy childhood. He discovered later that the colonel had won him in a game of stud at a house of frolic in New Orleans.

By the time he was in his early teens, Miller was a pro. He loved the life of the riverboats, those majestic floating palaces with their ornate saloons, sweeping decks, exquisite architecture and decoration. The clients were perfect: wealthy planters always willing to place a thousand or two on the turn of a card, a single roll of the dice, while overhead the lazy whirring of the ceiling fans emphasized the measured pace and stateliness of the great vessels as they swept grandly along the wide, wide waters through the heart of the wonderful new country.

Later there had been the trains. Less grand, to be sure, and more quickly paced, but thrilling in their race across the enormous land, with the all-night games from which men emerged to a new day red-eyed, tired, yet having satisfied something that only the game could feed, the game of chance.

But now, leaning against the wagon wheel, his long legs stretched out before him, while he dealt himself a hand of solitaire on the board he held on his lap, he took a moment to look up at the long, tingling light slipping over the land, drawing in toward the great shouldering hills across the river. "Soft, soft the light of even; soft the cheek of my beloved." Miller Muldoon was nothing if not a poet and a rogue.

And Miller told himself that he was getting old. He had never known his actual age, nor had his alleged parent, the Colonel, but to his own style of reckoning he placed himself only a year or two short of seventy. Not that it mattered, for he had all his faculties well in hand, and he was nimble. Only he had that feeling, the slowness in his bones and muscles, what seemed to be a thickening of the blood, and mostly an occasional rasping in the lungs. He told himself again as he reached into his shirt pocket for a cigar that he was bound to go out a lunger.

Ah, it was good! Quality Havana! There were only a few left in the box inside the wagon, and he would savor them. He smiled as his hand of solitaire worked out and, picking up the cards, he shuffled.

And yes, he'd had women. Young ones. Right now, the youngest of any. A girl, really. He had found her in Montana, Red Lodge or someplace, in the cabbage patch. Like the colonel before him he had educated the child. Got her books. Read to her. Taught her to read. Just like the colonel had done. With the added skill of the bed. His smile broadened as his nimble and vivid thoughts played over those shining moments of his colorful past. Just then he heard the step coming around the Conestoga and he knew it was John Slocum.

"I trust your hand has not lost its skill, Reverend." Slocum's green eyes were smiling as he regarded the man on the ground who was so obviously enjoying his cigar.

"A touch of the brew, Slocum?" Muldoon canted his head, squinting against the singeing light of the sun as it cut right across the team's rumps, blazing onto his face and hands. "The divine curse ennobles those who partake in moderation. Did you know that?"

Slocum nodded. "I do now. You know, it pleases me to see a man of God who isn't afraid to touch the bottle or a deck of cards."

Muldoon chuckled. "Even a man of God who isn't, eh? But no matter. One must know one's adversary." And with superb humor Muldoon allowed his body to bend in unctuous reverence as he reached into the blanket lying on the ground beside him, brought out a bottle, and uncorked it. "How else can one understand the poor, wretched sinner?"

He passed the bottle to his companion, who had squatted near him.

"I'm concerned about you and Ava," Slocum said

as, with his eyes watering, he handed the bottle back.

"Is it the redskins or the bandits?"

"The LeForts mostly, but the Indians, too."

Muldoon's lips pursed both in appreciation of the drink and Slocum's concern. "Desperadoes. But I know you will make it to Kansas, and I appreciate your taking us along with you. I only ask what I can do to help."

"Ava says you're a pretty fair shot."

"The girl is too modest on my behalf, sir. I happen to be an ace with rifle or handgun." He cocked his head at Slocum. "You suggest that I instruct her?"

Slocum nodded. "We need all the firepower we can get."

"Actually, I have already begun. Ava is an able student."

Slocum was eyeing the older man carefully, waiting for the moment to say what was really on his mind.

"I've another question, Reverend. It's about those Indians. The four who rode up to your wagon that day I ran into you in the meadow."

"A scary moment, I must say, Slocum. I was damn glad to see you."

Slocum, still squatting, shifted his stance a little, his eyes looking over the other's face as he spoke now.

"They were asking for whiskey, you'll remember."

"That is correct, sir." Catching something in Slocum's tone, Muldoon cut his eye quickly toward the man beside him.

"And did you have any?"

"But of course not! And certainly not for the Indians. Giving or selling whiskey to the redskins is against the law. You know that, sir!" His indignation thundered out and he shook his head vigorously, the slight wattles at his throat waggling like a rooster's.

But Slocum was closer than the old man's shadow. "I wasn't asking if you *sold* any, but whether you *had* any."

"Only for my personal, medicinal use, Slocum. Why are you questioning me like this?"

Slocum leaned toward him now. "You sure? What about those cases stacked behind your organ?"

Muldoon's eyes suddenly became milky with sightlessness. "Cases?"

"What have you got in them?"

"That is medicine, sir, in those cases. The former owner of the Conestoga wagon sold patent medicine, besides preaching the gospel. The man, as you may or may not know, died suddenly. His widow was in dire straits, and we—I—came to her rescue by purchasing the team and wagon and the organ. Indeed, I spent nearly all my small fortune on the transaction and so kept the medicine as a possible means of earning my living should the necessity arise."

"Medicine?"

"Dr. Rimbo's All-Purpose Health Elixir. Prevents anything. Cures anything. There is nothing like it."

"I'd like to see a bottle up close," Slocum said.

"Sir, you are drinking it right presently." Muldoon reached down. "Here, have another draught. It's likely to come chilly this night."

"Jesus Christ." Slocum stared, reaching out to accept the bottle. Uncorking, he sniffed. "It is pure whiskey," he said.

"Plus the secret formula."

He had to hand it to the Reverend; the man could have argued it straight as a string with Gabriel himself. "Those Indians thought you were a whiskey wagon bringing liquor out to the tribes," Slocum said.

"I'd no notion of that. On my honor as a man of God... well, as a gentleman and a scholar, sir!" He brought the last few words out with a firm rush, his cheeks coloring with emotion.

"Do you know how whiskey affects the Indians? Have you any notion of that? It drives them plumb crazy? They can't handle it. They go berserk!"

"Sir, you were there in the meadow. Did you see any of that merchandise pass between myself and those four redskins?"

Slocum had to admit that he had not.

Muldoon, his jowels quivering with feeling, brought in his clincher. "For God's sake, man, you don't believe I'd let that good whiskey... uh, medicine and health balancing agent fall into the hands of those savages, do you, sir? After all, I'm reaching the shores of seventy myself, and I have need of the equalizing fluid as I face my declining years!" His eyes pierced Slocum, shining like two torches leading the army of destiny across the great continent itself. Then he went on more softly, the words carved in sincerity, "Slocum, on my honor, I had no notion of those cases when I offered to buy the wagon from that poor and sudden widow. She told me it was patent medicine—which by Jehovah it is!—and I do believe that was how the Reverend himself saw it—as stock in trade. Believe me, sir. Believe me!"

"Give me one of those Havanas," Slocum said.

Muldoon's fingers whipped to his shirt pocket. "Forgive my oversight, sir. It's the least I can do."

Slocum bit the little bullet of tobacco out of the end, struck a lucifer, and lighted the cigar. The two of them bathed in the moment of supreme pleasure as he blew out the first fragrant cloud of smoke.

"Muldoon, I know you. But right now I don't really

give a shit about the whiskey. We have got action coming up, and I mean right now."

"I am with you, sir."

"So we will dump the whiskey."

All the blood suddenly drained from Muldoon's wrinkled face. He was white as death. "Surely you are funning me!"

"I'll let you keep a couple of bottles for yourself. But the rest gets dumped. We get in trouble, those bottles could fall into the wrong hands." And, standing up, he called out, "Denny, Harrigan!" As the men approached from where they had been hunkered by the campfire, he turned back to Miller Muldoon. "Two bottles, Reverend. For medicinal purposes."

It was the night following his conversation with Muldoon that Slocum, returning to his bedroll after checking the herd and the picket riders, found the girl waiting.

"You're up late," he said, speaking softly even though they were beyond the edge of the campsite and out of hearing of any of the men.

"I've been wanting..." she started to say, when he stepped closer and put his arms around her, his mouth sinking into hers. Their tongues drove at each other as their lips devoured the moment. At last, gasping for air, she pulled her mouth away.

"I can't do it. I'm too sore down there. Oh, God, I want you...!"

And then she was on her knees, her fingers pulling at his trouser buttons, then tugging, panting for breath as she grabbed his rigid member and pulled it out of his pants. Slocum felt his knees give and he put his hands on her shoulders to steady himself as she took his great organ into her mouth.

He was too big for her to take all of it and so she

grabbed him down at the base, gripping with her fist and stroking, her hand bobbing back and forth in time with her head as she sucked furiously. With her other hand she covered his balls, squeezing, playing her fingers on them, until he thought he would go out of his mind.

Finally he could stand it no longer. He sank down onto his back while she mounted him between his spread legs, now pulling down his trousers, yet not missing a stroke with either her mouth or her pumping fist.

Meanwhile, he had pulled down the top of her dress and had both breasts in his hands, rubbing the nipples, which were as big as the ends of his little fingers, squeezing them. She sucked greedily, and it seemed at one point to Slocum that she was going to choke as she took him all the way down her throat. He could hold it no longer and at last he came in a tremendous series of spurts. Together they thrashed until the very last, the ultimate, most exquisite drop.

They lay limp and ecstatic alongside each other. He was limp as a wet cloth; he had given everything from his whole body. Suddenly she raised up, coughing and choking. For a moment he was alarmed, but she subsided, laughing now as he patted her on the back solicitously.

"I'm all right—all right," she gasped. She leaned over him, pressing her wet lips on his, then raising to whisper, "My God, I thought you were going to drown me!"

"Maybe I will next time."

"Next time I want it inside me. It was just—I don't know. Tonight I wanted it like this."

"We could be greedy and have it both ways," he said.

She was tickling his ear with the tip of her tongue.

"You might be getting drowned sooner than you reckon on," he said, as his hand reached down into her drawers.

He felt her body tighten.

"I'm sorry, John. It's taking time to get over it."

"I know." He turned toward her and caressed the side of her face.

For a long moment they lay in silence. He must have fallen asleep, for suddenly he came awake. She was kneeling beside him in the dark, though her outline was clearly visible as she bent down to his growing member. Now slowly she began to lick his shaft, which was again rigid and wholly eager for her. He felt the moan of ecstasy running through his whole body as her lips sank down on him and her tongue continued to lick.

Dinwiddie carefully sliced himself a hefty chew of tobacco and, lifting it on the blade of his skinning knife, took it neatly into his mouth, clomping down on it with his brown and yellow-streaked teeth.

He felt better now in the dawn as he watched the cattle getting to their feet, the riders rousing them, moving them into the lines for the day's drive.

Slocum had told him to start the herd at daybreak and to keep going until he came to Buffalo Point just south of the Canadian, and that he would meet him there.

Wincing, he pressed the knuckles of his right hand hard against his game leg, just at the hip joint where the limb met his torso. Bending in the saddle, his wrinkles deepened in his effort to ease the pain.

Shit take it, a man got old! And he pushed at the joint again, and something released. Funny, for elsewise, he felt young, still felt the hunger for Nellie, and getting more so lately. And suddenly he was seeing her in his mind's eye, pulling off her shift, her drawers, and gazing—with his own body quivering with desire—at the dark, thick bush between her legs. And reaching over and fondling it, feeling the rich wetness. He drove the thoughts from the mind, kicking his big sorrel horse forward.

His thoughts changed abruptly as he forced them away from Nellie, but they didn't stop. And he was back to that bright day all that time ago in Toro Wells when he'd been the law and the Hogan boys had ridden in.

Hogan, all guts and leather, looking like he'd been stretched through a knothole, with a face like a hawk and eyes like a hungry rattler. And Daddy. Big Daddy LeFort. All meat, and a face looking like it had been marinated in beef brine. You could have struck a lucifer on him without making a mark. Both of them grease with the guns. Even now, even after all these years, he couldn't figure how he'd got away with it.

Course, he'd had the sawed-down Greener. But even so, if Daddy hadn't slipped in that pile of fresh horseshit at the critical moment it would have been a different story. He'd caught the two of them, and Roy Hames and Jastrow had gotten the rest.

It had shaken him. It had shaken him every now and again since, for it had been that moment, when he was almost a split second slow... and Daddy would have got him excepting for that wet pile of manure.

And now, these years later, he hadn't gotten any faster. In fact, he was slower. He knew it. Not so sure? He didn't know. But he would for sure have to watch it. He was no kid now. And Gans LeFort and his brothers would surely be as good, if not better, than Daddy. But Dinwiddie didn't like the occasional twinges in his hip, and he for sure didn't like the stiffness that came now and again in his right hand. It was at Slocum's suggestion that he had started practicing with his left.

"You might never get that fast with your other hand," his trail boss had told him. "But, for one thing, it'll take the pressure off your depending on your right. And you never know. You tell me Daddy LeFort slipped in a pile of wet horseshit. The next man might lose himself by getting a sudden itch up his ass."

In the hazy shimmering gray of pre-dawn, Slocum and two of his Arapaho scouts silently entered the muddy red waters of the Canadian River, a mile east of Carpenters Pass. As they reached the north shore, they remained on their bellies, inching their way slowly across the red sand.

On the rocky ground, they scrambled to their hands and knees, and then, crouching, moved swiftly through the darkness. And as dawn broke they were high among the rocks, looking down at Carpenters Pass below and a mile to the east.

Signaling to Bear Sings and Kicking Horse to stay where they were, Slocum snaked forward using his elbows and knees. It took a while, and he had to be especially careful about outriders. He didn't make a sound, trying to move in such a way that not even the air would be disturbed. A long while later he was on a sharp ridge overlooking a coulee next to Carpenters Pass.

Below him thirty men were seated around two campfires, wolfing food from tin plates. Near one fire he spotted Dutch Dillman, while at the other he recognized the great hulk of Gans LeFort. Gans was wearing a wide black sombrero, a black flannel shirt, and expensive Mexican trousers. An equally huge man was sitting at his right, but Slocum couldn't see his face, which was mostly hidden by an equally large black sombrero. One of the brothers, no doubt, he decided.

He made an effort to estimate the guns. There was no question but that the LeForts and their henchmen were massively armed.

As he watched an Indian scout—one of Little Coyote's band—rode up to the circle and dismounted in front of Gans. He pointed in the direction of Buffalo Point and began signing to Gans. But it was another man, on Gans's left, a big man with a red bandanna tied around his head, who conversed with the Indian, also using his hands. They were speaking as well, but Slocum couldn't hear the words. He could, however, read at least some of the signing, though it was difficult to see from his hidden position in the rocks above. The gist was that the scouts had located the Dinwiddie herd which was approaching Buffalo Point and would soon be at Carpenters Pass.

This news was greeted with shouts of laughter as the man beside Gans translated it to the gathering. Slocum barely caught one or two words. There was no question in his mind that this was indeed a perfect spot for the rubout. The KC wouldn't have a chance.

When he got down to Dinwiddie at Buffalo Point, he related quickly what he had seen.

"Beautiful!" the cattleman commented sardonically. He wagged his head. "You tell me they got thirty men and artillery fit for a army! And plus Indians! And we got eleven, plus a old man and a young woman and four Arapahoes. Shit! We will be just like all the others—huh! Those men there could wipe out the whole of the United States Cavalry in that place and not lose a man!"

"That's about the way they're thinking," Slocum agreed. "There is only one thing they maybe haven't figured on, though."

"And what is that?" Dinwiddie's sarcasm was like a rusty knife. "Help from the Almighty? We could carry that organ in there and them hymn books and sing and pray them to allow us through!" He threw out his hands and stomped around in a small circle, then suddenly faced Slocum again. "What do you mean, there is one thing they haven't figured on?"

"We have got small chance against that setup," Slocum agreed, saying it slowly, as though the words were following his thoughts and had a deeper meaning.

Dinwiddie snorted down his long nose. "I could of told you that back in San Antone, young feller."

"And the LeForts figure now more than ever we don't have a chance. I watched them there. I could tell that's how they were thinking. Lots of confidence. Some of them were even drinking. I think we've got a chance."

Dinwiddie stood swing-hipped, his hands in his back pockets, elbows out, and let a rush of air through his pursed lips. "So, how do you see it, General?" And the long, lean, lonely cattleman looked at Slocum plumb center.

"They figure they will ambush us just like they did the others," Slocum said calmly, ignoring Dinwiddie's impatience and sardonic humor. "So maybe we have to ambush them."

The cattleman's eyebrows shot up. "How'n hell we going to do that? They got more than twice what we have, plus who knows how much in guns and ammo! And plus, we have got them two thousand head of ornery Texas brutes. Tell me, while we are doing all this ambushing, who is going to wrangle them critters?"

Suddenly Dinwiddie's wrinkles gave way as his whole face cleared, a thought striking him. "I about forgot! You went to see that Injun—Yellow Eagle! You expecting him to help us? Hell, you know if he ever got involved in this shebang the army'd be up his ass so quick he wouldn't have time to say how-de-do! Besides, none of them got guns. The army took all their guns!"

Slocum was already holding up his hands to stem the rush of words from the excitable Dinwiddie. "Listen! Just remember one thing. Yellow Eagle wants to stop the whiskey coming into the Territory. And he figures we can help him by getting the LeForts out of the country some way or other."

"I understand, God damn it! And you are saying he can help us fight 'em. But how? God damn it, how?"

Slocum looked down at the palm of his big hand, spat in it, and rubbed his palms together, the way a man does before he takes up an axe or a shovel. He squinted close at the gingery Dinwiddie. "Tomorrow morning I am taking one hundred longhorns through Carpenters Pass."

The cattleman's jaw dropped open like a little door, but Slocum went on before he could speak. "I'll take four swing riders with me, plus the four Arapahoes. We get across there'll be four men sent up to the rocks at the top of the pass; two on each side. They'll be above the LeForts. The other four and myself will push the cows through; the LeForts thinking the whole herd is coming."

"And what'll I be doing with the other nineteen hundred longhorns?"

"You and the rest of the men, plus Muldoon and the girl will drive the herd west to Skin Creek Crossing; and *that's* where you'll cross the Canadian."

"You mean, while the LeForts are crossfiring you and the one hundred head, you'll have men crossfiring them from the top of the pass, and also below on the flanks!"

"It'll be a double ambush."

"Jesus!" Dinwiddie spat swiftly, without missing a beat, and said, "And where do the Arapahoes and Yellow Eagle come in?"

"Wherever we'll find a place for them, I guess," Slocum said drily. "It'll be handy to have them around, in any case."

"I hope they remember whose side they're on."

Slocum shifted his Stetson hat so that it was more forward on his head. "So do I," he said.

His plan was only half-formed, for it would eventually depend on how the action went; and he had no idea where Yellow Eagle's warriors could help, if indeed the chief would go along with him. But two days ago he had sent the scout Tail to Yellow Eagle, keeping Quick Walker close beside him. It was still dark when the men started the cattle out of Buffalo Point and by the time the first sign of dawn came into the sky, Slocum and his scouts and four drovers had started their hundred longhorns crossing the Canadian single file near Carpenters Pass. The riders kept the cattle strung out, hollering and riding back and forth loudly to give the impression of a herd of two thousand. To the west, Dinwiddie and his crew drove the bulk of the KC cattle toward Skin Creek Crossing.

Once across the river, Slocum and his men drove the longhorns over the half-mile stretch to the actual mouth of Carpenters Pass. Two of the riders and two Indian scouts dismounted and began scrambling up the rock cliffs, a pair of men on each side of the pass.

Slocum and the remaining men drove the cattle into the pass, still maintaining single file, making extra noise to give the impression of more longhorns than there actually were. The sun was already burning down, and Slocum searched the rocks above for some movement that would tell him the battle was starting.

He didn't have to wait. A rifle roared from the rocks above and a bullet cut the air near his right shoulder. He went head-first off his horse, rolling over on his side as bullets clipped the rocks around him. Reaching the shelter of a big rock, he waited only a moment to get his bearings, then crawled up to a ledge that hung above the pass.

From the rocks high up on the two hills now came the crack of rifles from the Arapaho scouts and the KC men, and as the four men at the opening of the pass fired at the LeForts simultaneously from the flanks, the would-be ambushers were themselves caught in a wicked double ambush.

The narrow pass was echoing with the roar of gunfire, the ricocheting of bullets, the shouting of men in anger and pain, while the smoke from the gunpowder added mightily to the confusion of the LeFort men.

A LeFort gunman suddenly screamed, dropping his rifle and clutching his head. Another, a tall, stringy man, doubled over, shot by Slocum in the stomach. Ike LeFort took a bullet in his hand. Shrieking his rage at the turn events were taking, he charged across to where Gans was shooting from behind a dead horse, bullets ripping his clothing.

"Gans, they've got us nailed down!" Ike shouted, his face twisted with pain, his smashed hand dripping blood.

"The hell they have!" his brother barked, firing at a gun flash on the other side of the pass. "Who's been hit?" he demanded, not seeing Ike's hand.

"Tolliver's done for, and they got Jake and Barlow. I think Ollie got nicked. I got this here. Gans, they somehow slickered us. That son of a bitch Slocum has slickered us again!"

In a fury his brother turned on him, but somehow controlled himself. "Where the hell are them goddamn Injuns!" he roared as Porky came up, dropping down behind the horse, into whose corpse someone high up was pouring bullets.

"They got me, boys!" It was Finn, crying out from several feet away. And, turning, his brothers saw him plummet out of a crevice of rock and spin down to the floor of the pass.

"God almighty!" Porky rose slightly and emptied his gun, to no apparent use.

"We got to get outta here!" snapped Gans. "We have got to haul ass!" He rose, but dropped down immediately as a wave of bullets tore his hat from his head.

"Gans!" It was Print crawling to his brothers on hands and knees. "That Injun..."

"Where is the son of a bitch!"

"There's a way out of the pass. C'mon!"

"Covering fire, you men!" Gans shouted to two of the gunslingers who were forted in the rocks above and to his left. "Banks, Harlet! Lay it on!"

And he turned, just as Ollie appeared, and the brothers raced after Print, who was following Little Coyote. Under a massive barrage of fire which hit nobody in the cliffs above or at the flanks, the LeForts made it to their horses and, mounting, swept down the narrow trail after Little Coyote and his band, now reduced to seven.

Outside the canyon, Gans called a halt. Behind them the battle was still on, with the hired LeFort men fighting for their lives.

"Gans, that son of a bitch only pushed a hundred head into the pass." Ollie pumped the words up past the pain in his chest as he tried to regain his breath. He had taken a bullet in the ribs.

"Where did you get that?"

"In the ribs," Ollie gasped bleakly.

"I mean, about the cattle, you asshole!"

"The Injun told me. The main herd's crossing down at Skin Creek."

"Boys, Finn's back at the pass." It was Ike, blood soaking through the rag he had wrapped around his hand.

"He is dead," snarled Gans. "You want to go back in there and get your ass shot off?" He spat furiously, yanking at his horse's mouth. "We are riding to Skin Creek!" And he spurred his horse into a high gallop, his brothers racing after him.

10

At Skin Creek Crossing Otis Dinwiddie and his crew were just starting the leaders across the Canadian River. Ava, riding the black gelding, and Miller Muldoon, astride a bay horse taken from the KC remuda, were helping to point them. The crossing was not difficult, for the water at that place was shallow. And the animals, having already refreshed themselves fully after the drought, were reasonably well behaved.

"We will head them directly north," Dinwiddie said. "We'll cut left of that hill yonder and through the valley bottom. That's good feed ahead, but keep pushing them, and keep them close together."

On Slocum's advice he had the men riding in pairs, with one man working the cattle, the other watching for trouble. The herd was almost completely across when Dinwiddie heard the horses. He could tell by the sound drumming through the ground that it was trouble.

"Turn them leaders!" he shouted. "Circle them in right by the river. Get the rest of the critters acrost!" He kicked his big sorrel back into the water and began hitting the brutes to move them.

"Work 'em into a circle. Make them mill! We'll use 'em as breastworks!" He booted the sorrel up out of the water and galloped after the leaders. "It's the LeForts!" he shouted. "Bunch 'em and let them mill!"

The leaders were already turned, the men clouting them with their lariat ropes and quirts; and Dinwiddie was even hitting them with the stiff wide brim of his Stetson hat.

"Stay mounted!" he shouted above the uproar. "And pick your shots. Don't waste anything on the sons of bitches!"

He raced the sorrel down the length of the herd, barking orders. "You men, watch the flanks. They'll see they can't shoot through all that beef, so they'll try a sweep around the ends. Keep that right flank nubbed tight to the river bank where it ain't shallow— I am saying, right where it is deep!"

A hail of rifle fire drowned out any further orders as the LeFort brothers plus Little Coyote and his men pounded across the open stretch of land. Reaching the end of the line, some of the Indians tried to cut around the cattle, but Dinwiddie's men had brought the beeves right up to the bank of the river, where the water was too deep for them to maneuver their horses.

Little Coyote rode boldly at the head of his men. He had painted his entire body yellow, and had red and green streaks painted on his white pony. Charging Thunder had covered himself with red and white hail spots and stripes, and his pony's face was decorated with red circles. Both he and his cousin were determined to count coup. They rode wildly, guiding their mounts with their legs, leaving their hands free to fire their guns, and presently their arrows.

Close by, Gans and Porky LeFort urged their horses to their utmost. Right behind them galloped four of their men. All were firing at will. A horse screamed suddenly and one of the gunmen toppled to the ground, only just clearing his legs from the falling animal in the nick of time. He rose instantly, firing, and winged one of the KC cowboys.

Suddenly Gans jerked back on his reins, leaning

his entire strength and weight against the drive of his galloping horse. In so doing he all but stood the dappled gray onto its hind legs.

"God damn it!" he roared. "Slocum has got to still be back at the pass!" And he pumped his arm up and down angrily, his face red with frustration. "By God, the son of a bitch has got to come here when he sees we took off after the cattle! Porky, you take them Injuns and Ollie over yonder by the willows. We'll set up a crossfire. Me and Ike and Print will be by the cutbank there. The rest of you spread out and move this goddamn herd out of the way. Don't forget, we want that son of a bitch Dinwiddie!"

By now the terrified cattle were starting to break and Dinwiddie realized that in only moments they would be running and he and the others would be exposed to the fire of the LeForts and Little Coyote's Arapahoes. And even now he could see more of the LeFort men riding in from Carpenters Pass to join Gans and his brothers.

Now the LeForts, under the lash of Gans, were concentrating their attack, aided by the Arapahoes and hired gunmen. Even though their forces had been decimated in the double ambush at the pass, they were still mustering superior numbers to the Dinwiddie crew.

Meanwhile, Young Denny had been killed, and a man named Ray lay dying, gutshot. Heavy Pete O'Hay had taken lead in both legs. He was lying on the ground, his back propped against a wheel of his chuck wagon, while Ava reloaded the Henry rifle for him and Miller Muldoon passed him the bottle. Heavy Pete's pain was thus muted with alcohol and the presence of Ava.

"God bless you!" he said to her as he shot to death a short man who was riding a big bay horse and carrying two empty holsters on his bony hips.

"There is justice, O Lord!" exclaimed Miller Muldoon, who lay on his stomach next to O'Hay, firing at the oncoming LeForts.

"Keep them critters bunched to the river!" roared Dinwiddie, though he knew it was hopeless; he was telling himself that in a few moments they would be spread over half the Indian Territory.

It was just then that he heard more firing from the other side of the river. To his astonishment, he saw Slocum and his men racing their horses along the opposite bank, firing at the LeForts, who were taken completely by surprise; now finding themselves caught once again in wicked crossfire between the Dinwiddie men and Slocum.

But Gans boldly whipped his big gray through a gap in the firing and the others followed, the running cattle offering them cover.

Slocum was still on the other side of the river, unable to cross because of the depth of the water. And Dinwiddie, watching the situation, realized that when Gans and his men rode out of range of Slocum's fire, they would have the distinct advantage with their superior numbers and firepower in facing first one group and then the other.

Some of the men were still trying to hold the cattle, but it was clearly hopeless. Dinwiddie was about to shout at them to give it up and dig in, when suddenly a shout reached him from across the river and he saw that Slocum had found a crossing. Now the firing intensified as Slocum and his men splashed through the water, firing at the LeForts, who now were only partially protected by the moving cattle.

Unaccountably, there was a sudden lull in the fighting, possibly because the beeves were in the lines of fire again; but whatever the reason, it was at this moment that there came the distinct and totally unexpected sound of an eagle-bone whistle.

And suddenly there were mounted Indians everywhere—shrieking, shooting their bows and arrows. Some were firing aged flintlocks as they raced around the churning longhorns who, given another minute, would surely stampede.

Slocum galloped his buckskin pony around to the other end of the herd as Dinwiddie, recovered from his surprise, urged the Indians and cowboys to hold the critters. But the cattleman swiftly realized that his trail boss had something else in mind, for Slocum was racing along the line of cows firing near their feet and over their heads, smashing at them with his quirt when his gun was empty and shouting to the riders to stampede them.

"What the hell . . . !" Dinwiddie started to roar, but then realized what was happening, as in only moments the entire herd had been pointed into a wedge by Slocum and the Arapahoes and was charging down upon the LeForts and their gunmen, who now had their backs to the river. The avalanche of beef bore all of them over the bank of the river and into the water.

Slocum, Dinwiddie, and their men were off their horses now and, protected by the cottonwoods and willows, were firing at the enemy at will.

Seeing that the LeForts were done for, Slocum gave orders to his Indian scouts to begin rounding up the cattle before they got too far. Bear Sings and Kicking Horse raced to where Yellow Eagle was sitting a blue roan horse on a rise of ground, flanked by two of his headmen. Receiving Slocum's message, the chief blew the eagle-bone whistle and gave orders to his warriors, who now began herding the cattle back toward the river.

There were a few survivors among the LeForts. Print, Ollie, and Ike had all been wounded, Ollie quite seriously. And as he stood knee-deep in the Canadian River between his brothers who were supporting him on either side, he began to sag. There was a trickle of blood coming out of his mouth; his face was the color of slate. Ike's hand, which had been shot up at Carpenters Pass, was a gleaming black-and-scarlet flag. He was holding his arm slightly away from his body as though he wanted to protect his clothing from that terrible hand. His color was not much better than that of his brother, for he too had lost a lot of blood. And now, both of them, with the battle over, had time to let their bodies take in the toll of their activities. Only Print remained wholly erect, though he had been shot in the leg. Only a flesh wound, but it had hampered his attempt to escape at the end. Seizing a horse, he had tried desperately to mount, but the wounded leg had foiled him and the horse had started to buck as Print's foot missed the stirrup. Print had been thrown and the wind knocked out of him. Now the three remaining brothers stood like a final fortress in the middle of the river. About half a dozen of the gunslingers had survived Carpenters Pass and the battle at the Canadian. These stood in disarray in the quiet, swirling river, which seemed to pay no attention whatsoever to its grisly guests. They stood in their battle-soaked clothes, which in some cases looked more substantial than the bodies they attempted to cover. But Gans and Porky had vanished.

Slocum ordered the remnants to unbuckle. As this was done, he turned his eyes on the KC hands. Three had been killed, Heavy Pete and two others wounded. Pete's legs were in poor shape, but Ava and Muldoon had made him comfortable. And to be sure, the "Reverend" was medicating himself as well as his patient. Both he and Ava were unscathed, for which Slocum was grateful.

"We'll be shorthanded getting them to Abilene," Dinwiddie said, his good eye observing the cattle being brought in by the Indians.

"We'll make it," Slocum said grimly. He was standing close to the edge of the river watching the three remaining LeForts struggling out of the water, wondering if they were going to make it. Suddenly he realized that one of the LeFort gunmen trudging out of the water directly behind the three LeForts was Dutch Dillman. He was only a couple of feet or so in back of Print LeFort.

The LeForts had stopped, gasping for breath, and Slocum could see that Ollie was about done for. And, in fact, he suddenly sagged out of his brothers' arms and lay down in the water. Ike bent over him.

"Ollie's dead," he said. They all heard him.

"You win this time, Slocum," Print said, his voice hard with hate. "Next time..."

"This *is* next time, LeFort. You're lucky I don't kill you. You and your brother get on and get out!" He turned his eyes on the hired gunmen. "You, too. I see a one of you, no matter where...here, in Abilene, in Frisco, no matter where...I will kill you. That's not a threat, it's a promise. Now git!"

But Dutch Dillman was not through. He held up his bandaged arm, which Slocum had pistol-whipped, as the little corps of wounded men started toward the riverbank again. "I will see you next time, Slocum. I still owe you for this!"

Slocum didn't answer. He watched Dillman lower his arm, reaching up with his left hand to support it. He hadn't realized how badly he had injured the kid, who was still partly hidden behind Print LeFort.

In the next split second he understood how close he had just come to making his last mistake. Swift as smoke, Dillman's other hand pulled the bandage from the hideout gun in his covered hand, and in the same flash Slocum saw Print drop his right arm to the man standing directly behind him.

But in that same instant a shot rang out from behind Slocum and Dutch Dillman collapsed forward, falling on his face in the water. In the same clap of sound, Slocum's right hand swept the .31 from its holster, thumbing it for speed and twisting his body to align his shot as Print LeFort came up with the gun that Dillman had passed him.

John Slocum was quicker. He shot Print LeFort right through the chest. As the last and present defender of the LeFort clan floundered right there in the Canadian River like a gnarled buffalo, he cursed Slocum.

"We're not through with you yet, Slocum!"

"*You're* through, mister. This was your 'next time.'"

And he watched Print LeFort slump dying into the river, as his wounded brother Ike, his face almost totally without blood, it seemed, sank down in the river with him.

Turning his head quickly to where the shot had come from behind him, Slocum saw Miller Muldoon lowering the Henry rifle with which he had killed Dillman.

Muldoon was still kneeling on one knee, his eyes gripping the half-submerged body of Dillman. His words came clearly to those around him.

"There is justice in this world...." And he dropped the rifle, and kneeling on both knees now, bowed his head. "There is justice!"

Slocum watched Ava walk over, kneel down beside him, and touch his shoulder with her fingers.

Miller Muldoon raised his head. "Jesus, Pete," he said, turning toward Heavy Pete O'Hay, "I need a shot of your medicine, by God!"

11

"Well, we busted the buggers," Dinwiddie said, and he blew his nose loudly in emphasis, canting his head to one side and pressing his thumb against one long nostril. The sound was short, emphatic, and even carried authority.

But Slocum was not convinced. "Don't be so sure," he declared. "Those boys don't give up easy. There is still Gans and Porky."

"I have not forgotten them, and I am ready for the both of them," Dinwiddie said. "But they will not have their family and friends along next time, is what I am saying."

One evening when they had driven the herd far up into Kansas, with the battle of Carpenters Pass gradually giving way in the men's thoughts and conversation to anticipation of Abilene, Slocum lay quietly on his bedroll, thinking of how the cattle trail the KC had blazed would now be a permanent route to the northern shippers. Dinwiddie and the KC were the first, and had made history. Not that he cared a damn about history, but it had been well worth it.

His thoughts slipped to Yellow Eagle, and he smiled, thinking of the scene just after the conclusion of the fight at the Canadian when the chief had pony whipped Little Coyote and Charging Thunder right in front of the tribe. It had been a moment! The chief would have normally delegated such a task to the Dog Soldiers, but he had taken the whip in his own hand

and meted the punishment. And right before the whites, too! Slocum had almost felt sorry for Little Coyote and his cousin.

Slocum grinned now, seeing in his mind's eye the energetic, dignified old man whipping those two young men back to their duty, insisting that they behave in a way becoming to the tribe. And they had taken it. It was a good thing to see, and for Slocum and probably for others, too, it had cleaned away many of the bad memories of that day of killing. It was good to see once again such a rare thing: a man of principle, insisting that the way of a man and a warrior be understood and followed.

When he had parted with Yellow Eagle, Slocum had said, "I hope we meet again, Yellow Eagle."

The chief had looked into him with his quiet, penetrating eyes, as a long moment of silence held them.

"If it is to be then we will meet again, Slow-Come. Yet, if we do not, it does not mean that we are separated. Our moment together will always be here, in this gentle evening, in this beautiful land."

After another long moment, Slocum said, "I am sure the whiskey peddling will stop now. Before he died, Ike LeFort told me it was them bringing it into the territory."

The chief said nothing, and Slocum realized that this man lived in the present. The matter was done; there was no point in even mentioning it. He had spoken of it so that it would be clear, and he wasn't sorry. But once again he appreciated how the Arapaho had reminded him of what was important: only what was necessary, the present moment, and the attention that was required in facing it totally. And it was just this he was going to need now, because it wasn't over. It wasn't anywhere near over.

• • •

He had closed his eyes and now he opened them. A soft wind stirred over the prairie, which lay golden in the dying sunlight. And he smelled the horses in the remuda nearby, listened to the tinkling of the grazing bell, the call of a scolding jay.

Her step was soft, but he heard it clearly, and he said, "I've been waiting for you."

"I hope it wasn't too long."

"It was just right."

She lay down beside him, both of them on their backs looking up at the velvet sky, holding hands as the light faded and the night came. Presently, without a word, they turned toward each other.

Her breath was warm on his face as she said, "It's been so very long a time."

"Never mind. We're here now."

"John..."

"Take it slow."

"All that trouble, the killing. Not just what happened to me and Miller. But the whole of it..."

"It's done now."

"These past days since we left all that...they've been good days. Only I'm still..."

"Raw?"

"Yes...a little." She reached up and touched his face with the tips of her fingers. "I'm sorry. Will you help me?"

He didn't answer. He simply moved toward her and kissed one of her eyelids, and then the other. And then slowly he began to take off her clothes.

"I want you to wash me clean," she said.

And then it was no longer possible to speak as their passion gently grew and at length took over and they lost all sense of time and place, of anything except their shared joy as their bodies moved in one rhythm, dancing together. His great organ drove into her while she spread herself to the utmost, writhing on its hard tip until finally each brought the other to the acme of pleasure, deeper and faster, until all awareness of anything was gone; this most exquisite slavery to their bodies was all there was in the whole world.

It was late when he walked her back to the wagon. Much later, some while before dawn, he awakened, knowing instantly that it was earlier than usual for him. He had the strange feeling that there was something out of place, something he couldn't narrow to a word. So after a moment he didn't try. He simply tried to experience it, feel it. And as the dawn came he knew they were being followed.

For Otis Dinwiddie the spring was the best time. He had always liked the warm weather coming after the long winter of cold and snow and blizzards. It was good to see the land greening up through the last of the snow and the hard sod. And he liked the way people were then: more alive, more fun to be with, though he knew himself as a dour man. But he liked others to make up for what he lacked. And then he liked best to be alone, too, lying under the stars listening to a coyote barking and watching the young moon climbing the sky and washing the rolling prairie in its soft light.

But now it was getting close to the first of May, the time when Eli Case expected the herd in Abilene. He wasn't as sure as Slocum that they would make it. He had ridden out with his trail boss, scouting for sign of the two remaining LeForts, Gans and Porky, but they had found nothing.

"A notion I had," Slocum said. "Felt it in my guts."

"I know how that is," Dinwiddie agreed. "Won't let you loose, but you can't get a rope on it."

It was a soft day, with the high clouds scudding across the sky, and now and then a random wind bending the trees and the tall grasses.

Now the two men rode in silence, and when they came to the creek Slocum suddenly drew rein. Dinwiddie, on the sorrel he favored, almost ran into the spotted horse's rump.

They were at the edge of the creek, where the thin water was lapping over some rocks. Dinwiddie saw that Slocum's eyes were on something, but he couldn't make out what. Slocum had swung out of his saddle, keeping his eyes right on whatever he was looking at. Ground-hitching his pony, he walked toward the water's edge and, squatting, picked up a stone and held it.

"Warm, is it?" Dinwiddie asked, joining him.

"No—But somebody built a fire. And they didn't scatter it right, or they were likely in a hurry." Slocum had released the hammer thong on his .31 and was now standing, but not quite fully erect, for he was searching the ground; now he began moving along the creek bank.

He stopped again and pointed to a bush that was right at the edge of the water. "Some berries been knocked off there," he said.

"Gans and Porky, you figger?"

"Hard to tell." He was moving upstream with Dinwiddie close behind him. All at once, he stopped dead in his tracks. Reaching out, he pulled a bent branch from a big bush. "And that horse is shod," he said, nodding toward a hoofprint at the edge of the water. "Got a loose shoe. I'd bet on it being the LeForts."

And then he added, "But they are for sure gone."

"You're not going after?"

"They'll be about; we'll meet up with them." He fell silent again as he studied the terrain, reading it more clearly now that he was more sure.

He continued to search the ground, the trees and bushes, the opposite side of the creek, going slowly, taking his time. A couple of hours passed.

Dinwiddie also studied it, finding the partial imprint of a boot heel. He was a good tracker, but not in Slocum's class. Slocum had tracked men, not just animals, and he knew what to look for.

At last he straightened up and lit a quirly, while his companion took out his chewing tobacco and cut a slice.

"They cut our trail," Slocum began. "Not hard to do, with what we're trailing. And then they followed for a spell."

"You think they'll keep following?"

"Maybe. It doesn't matter. The thing is, they're not hanging around close, is the way I see it. I will bet they've circled wide around the herd so as to get ahead of us. But I'll check that out tomorrow. There isn't enough daylight left now."

"Why did they do that? They could have stayed and tried to bushwhack us."

"They could have, but they didn't." He squinted at the sun, which was just reaching the distant hills that made the horizon. "Could be they've got a reason for getting ahead of us."

"Like planning a party?"

A grim smile crossed Slocum's face as he took off his hat and adjusted it more forward on his brow. "We'll shortly find out, I've a notion."

They rode back in silence, reaching the campsite around sundown, when the tired men were stripping the gear from their tired and sweaty horses. Dinwiddie and Slocum joined them as they washed up and then ate a leisurely supper.

Slocum sat quietly not far from the fire while the men swapped a few lies about their experiences with bad horses, good liquor, and reluctant women. Then it was time to heave their bedrolls from the chuck wagon and bed down for the night.

He continued to sit by the fire, idly watching Miller Muldoon and the wounded yet active Heavy Pete playing poker with a couple of men on a saddle blanket spread out in the campfire light.

Then it was time to turn in.

That night Ava was again waiting for him when he reached the place where he had spread his bedroll.

For a while they lay beside each other on top of his bedding, fully clothed. It was peaceful, and he felt a sweetness coming from her and running through him. They just lay like that, without doing anything; just being together. And then—it was a good while later—she got up and went back to her wagon. Slocum felt a good feeling inside him.

He slept only a few hours, and in the early predawn he rose and rolled his bedding and rode the buckskin out from camp. The sky was lightening as he picked up the trail of Gans and Porky LeFort.

"I still don't see why we don't just pick off those two sons of bitches, God damn it!" Porky LeFort leaned forward and poked the small campfire, then reached for his tin cup of coffee. When his brother still said nothing, he went on. "Easy enough to slip up on them, like at night, or early when the camp's still asleep, and drygulch the bastards. We'd be long gone before anybody'd come after."

His brother Gans, squatting by the fire, suddenly belched. "Dumb. That is not the way to do it. Not the way at all. For Christ's sake, Porky, don't you know that son of a bitch Slocum by now *knows* we have cut his trail!" He belched again, more softly this time. "He is smart enough to have slickered us more than once, so he is smart enough to know we are not heading for Texas or somethin'."

"I know the fucker is smart. I am saying that is why we should rub him out fast, and not waste time farting around."

"That is what he is expecting, you asshole! He'll be just waiting for us!"

"Aw shit!" Porky's jaw fell to his collarbone.

"But he is not smart enough to slicker us again! I want him to know that, Porky my boy. And I want you to understand it likewise!"

"Then what are you figuring on, Gans? The two of us against the whole bunch of them, plus maybe that tribe of Indians?" Porky shifted his weight, feeling his left shoulder with his fingers, carefully. He'd been wounded and had lost some blood.

"How's that?" Gans didn't answer his brother's question, but nodded toward the shoulder. "Bleeding stopped?"

"It is all right. Stiff. Lucky it wasn't my right, my gun arm." Porky poked at the fire again. "I'm for heading straight on up to Abilene, laying for Slocum and Dinwiddie there. Or, better, rubbing them out fast right now and then be shut of it."

"There is the herd of cattle," his brother pointed out. "They get to Abilene, we are done for."

Porky nodded. He was reluctant, but he had to

admit the sense of what his brother was saying. "If we knock off Dinwiddie and Slocum, then the cattle will be easy. There'll be no one to whipsaw that outfit. They hardly got enough men now."

Porky caught the lazy smile stealing into his brother's eyes.

"Have you noticed how dry it's been getting this past day or two?" Gans's two upper front teeth and a gap where the two lower were missing suddenly appeared in his hairy face.

"It ain't rained in a long spell."

"That's what I am saying."

"So what is that meaning?"

"Remember those days a while back when there was no water, the waterholes dried up, the wallows and the creeks, and those beeves were really hurting?"

"Sure. But it ain't like that now."

"It is getting like that. Shit, Porky, just feel it." Gans held up his big forefinger, wiggling it just a little, feeling the dryness in the air.

Porky shrugged with his good shoulder, but the effort moved his other one and his wound hurt him. He winced. "It's dry, but not all *that* dry. So what are you saying there, anyways?"

"Porky, it is dry." Gans opened his eyes very wide in emphasis so that they popped at his brother like two huge marbles. "That *is* what I am getting at." And, reaching into the pocket of his hickory shirt, he brought out a cigar stub and a lucifer. Putting the cigar between his teeth, he struck the match and sat watching the flame. He lit the cigar, then continued holding the match in front of him as the flame consumed the wood. Porky watched the grin spreading over his big face.

When he finally dropped the burned piece of match,

Gans said, "We will head for Abilene, and we will celebrate in Abilene." His eyes were on their back trail. He was looking in the general direction of the KC herd.

"Celebrate what? For Christ's sake, Gans, what the hell you talking about?" Porky's voice rose, sharp with anger.

But Gans didn't answer. He was chuckling softly to himself. And for a moment Porky wondered if his brother was getting lost in his head. He'd only been scratched along his cheek and on his wrist, but the strain of the fighting might have got to him. Yet he knew it couldn't be that. He knew Gans was tough as stretched animal gut. Nothing ever bothered Gans. But, by God, there he was grinning to himself about something or other; and he hadn't been drinking, even; not a drop, as far as Porky could tell.

Porky sat there by the almost-dead fire, watching his brother, wondering what could be going on with him, but then dropping that—for he never did think of anything for any real length of time—and thinking now of getting to town and getting some drinks and some girls. That was more like it. But even that didn't last, and he was thinking of Dinwiddie and Slocum and how they would get the two of them, but pretty damn directly. Not to let it wait long.

Now he watched his brother strike another lucifer and sit watching it burn down between his fingers before tossing it into the fire, then another one. Gans was still grinning, and gradually Porky began to catch on. Gradually he began to see his brother's plan.

"Let's have a drink on it," he said. And he rose, his own big grin joining his brother's, and crossed to where his saddlebag was leaning against a tree.

They continued to sit there, drinking, now and

again saying something or other, chewing on some beef jerky and drinking coffee, now and then taking a pull from the whiskey bottle. Gradually they grew sleepy.

The moon rose as the two men lay on their saddle blankets on the ground.

"Gans..."

"Yeah."

"That's a good idea you got."

"I know that."

Another long moment of silence fell between them, but neither was sleeping.

"Gans..."

"Yeah..."

"Where the hell is Goose?"

"How the fuck do I know?"

"I wish he was here."

"Shut up!"

"Gans, I'm going out to get that son of a bitch Dinwiddie. I am sick of this waiting shit!"

"Shut up!"

Otis Dinwiddie raised the big Colt slowly, held it at arm's length for a second, two, and squeezed the trigger. The bottle, hanging from a string tied to the branch of a cottonwood tree, exploded.

"Good enough," Slocum said, coming up behind him as Dinwiddie lowered his arm.

"Still feels funny doin' it with my left hand."

"Now you got to shoot the string," Slocum said.

A thin smile sliced across the cattleman's wrinkled face. "I probably could've done that in the old days, when my right hand was still my right hand."

"It'll come. Just keep working at it." Slocum stood squinting at the older man. "Course, the best lawmaker of the lot is what you caught Daddy LeFort with."

"The cut-down Greener."

Slocum nodded, taking out a wooden lucifer and sticking it in his mouth to hold like a toothpick. "That poor son of a bitch. Not much left to plant, I don't doubt."

"He was a tough one, LeFort. I told you he didn't die till he got home and got into bed. About a week after those blue whistlers ventilated him."

Slocum nodded, remembering the story Dinwiddie had told him the first day he'd met him on the cattle drive. "I guess the two of them are still game to equalize that for their pa."

"Gans or Porky—one."

"Or both. I haven't noticed those boys being particular how they rub a man out."

A wry grin appeared on Dinwiddie's leathery face. Now he walked over to a second bottle that was hanging from a string tied to another tree and pushed it with his hand so that it began to swing. Returning to where Slocum was standing, he stood for a moment watching the bottle. Then he drew, took aim, and fired. This time he missed.

"Shit! Shit take it!"

"Don't waste your time talking about it," Slocum snapped, hard. "Hit the son of a bitch."

This time Dinwiddie hit the still moving bottle plumb center.

Lowering the sixgun, he said, "I owe you one there, Slocum. Talking can kill a man, for sure."

Slocum was grinning. "Thing is to keep shooting. You never know what can happen. Try with your right hand, now."

This time it was Slocum who walked forward and

tied a fresh bottle to each string, so that there were two. Then he started them swinging and walked quickly back to join Dinwiddie. "One with each hand now."

Dinwiddie was standing easy, his arms at his sides, his hands loose, near each holstered sixgun.

"Now," Slocum said. And the cattleman drew, shattering the first bottle with his left, but missing the second with his right hand. Though he got it on his third shot.

Lowering his guns, then holstering them, he spat and turned a rueful gaze on his companion. "Felt freer on the left than the right, by golly."

"You have got to stop thinking about it. Never mind whether it's left or right, your good hand or your bad hand. You've got to figure there's no distance between you and what you are hitting. You understand? You're not *going* to hit anything, you *are* hitting it. It's that fast. You don't let anything come between you and the target. Nothing. Not a thought! Otherwise you'll miss."

Dinwiddie spat casually at a clump of fresh cow manure. "Set 'em up again," he said.

This time he missed everything.

"That's enough," Slocum said. "You can try too hard. You've got it. I can see you've got it. So just let it cook inside you a while. It's there, and when you need it, it'll come."

"By God, you got more confeedience than I got myself," Dinwiddie said.

"No, I've got more confidence than you have in your head. Only you're not going to shoot anybody with your head or your thoughts or your mouth. It'll be with what you got in your body." Slocum walked forward and started the two bottles moving.

He stood beside Dinwiddie and loosened the hammer thong on the .31 Colt. "You call it," he said.

They stood side by side for a couple of moments.

"Now," Dinwiddie whispered.

Almost before the soft sound of that single word had died, Slocum had drawn and shot one bottle, then the other.

"Now!" he said, catching Dinwiddie in surprise. The cattleman drew and shot the neck of the first bottle that was still swinging slightly on the end of the string. But he missed the second.

Slocum was grinning. "That's good enough, old timer. You are all right."

Dinwiddie was grinning ruefully. "You caught me there, Slocum. I wasn't expecting you to call."

"That's just why I called you. Never expect what's going to happen. Never! Because what does happen is always something else."

"I owe you again."

"You can pay that one back to the LeForts," Slocum said. He looked at the sky for a long moment. "You know, it ain't getting any cooler. I do hope we are not in for another big heat."

"It is getting dry," Dinwiddie observed as they walked slowly toward the chuck wagon.

Slocum said, "I'll be riding out to see what water there is ahead. But first I'm going to check my loads."

As they approached the chuck wagon he saw Ava in the distance walking toward the Conestoga, and suddenly he felt his passion rising. He would be looking forward to nightfall, he knew.

With Heavy Pete out of action, Ava had taken over the duties of cook, assisted by a young man named

Jeff, who also wrangled the horses. They were a week out of Abilene now, and it looked as though they would meet Eli Case's deadline. Still, the heat did not let up, and even seemed more intense. The men were exhausted and the cattle weren't much better off. There had been no rain, and the land was beginning to crackle. At this point, their experience with the drought down in the Indian Territory had been a lot more severe. Now, even though the creeks were low in water, and the buffalo wallows were dried up, they weren't totally without water. But Slocum ordered rationing and cautioned the men about fire.

"We had better reach civilization soon," Miller Muldoon observed to his companion on the other side of the horse blanket, "or we will be in big trouble."

"How so?" Heavy Pete O'Hay studied his cards from beneath raised eyebrows, but his attention had been caught by the seriousness in the Reverend's tone.

"We are running low on Dr. Rimbo's All-Purpose Health Elixir, O'Hay. That is not good." He wagged his head, his wattles whipping. "That is not good at all." He checked his hole card and said, "I'll raise you."

But O'Hay threw down his hand in disgust. "Never was good at the cards, Muldoon. Nor the dice."

"Takes practice, my lad," Muldoon said softly, collecting the cards and fitting them so he could shuffle. "I am but an amateur myself, but I am a devoted amateur; therefore, you might say I carry the advantage over an opponent like yourself."

"Cards is fun. Especially poker." Heavy Pete shifted his enormous weight. He was seated in his customary position whenever they made camp, with his back against the wagon wheel, his injured legs stretched out in front of him. Ava attended to him regularly, and he was on the mend. The Reverend took care of his social needs, plying him with medicine and practicing his trade as well as imparting the lore of the gaming table to his new companion.

But Heavy was glum. "Thought at one time I might get myself into the cards and dice, work my way into a new line of work. Not so rough on a man as this trail herding."

"You must be patient," the Reverend said mildly. "I myself, amateur that I am, have studied the game for years." He paused, holding his forefinger beneath his nose to stop a sneeze. Then, releasing, he sighed. "I am also getting low on Havanas, but we will enjoy a smoke now, even so." He drew two fine cigars from his coat pocket and passed one to Heavy Pete O'Hay, whose big face lit up in anticipation.

"Anybody can take to the game. Anybody, man or woman," Miller Muldoon said as he shuffled, rambling over the words as though in a way he were sorting them out while looking for something else. "Why, I even know women gamblers, good ones." He paused, his eyes twinkling, to the surprise of Heavy Pete, who had never seen such an expression before on his companion's face.

The Reverend chuckled in reminiscence. "Lovely lady, one in particular. Mary Louise, her name was. Up north in the Sierras. She could slicker the best of 'em. Rich, she was, and good-lookin', but I don't know of any man made it into her drawers. She minded herself, Mary Louise did."

He put down the deck of cards and began preparing his cigar, biting away the little bullet of tobacco, licking the end so that it would be damp and soft, holding it to his nose, and rolling his eyes in pleasure. Then finally striking a match, letting it burn a moment before touching the treasured tobacco, then lighting.

Much of the ritual was lost on the likes of Heavy Pete O'Hay, who clearly hailed from coarser stock. But Pete went through the same motions, perhaps hoping to find something new for his life. He found nothing special for himself in aping the Reverend's actions, but he did discover a superb smoke. And that, after all, was the point.

"Mary used to play a special. It was a real jim-dandy—all in the shuffle, you might say. Want to hear about it?"

Heavy Pete didn't have time to say yea or nay before the Reverend was hurrying on.

"I'm telling you this without fear you'd copy it. You couldn't, since it takes a real professional to pull it off. But I tell it to you just to indicate—I say indicate, sir!—the wholesome beauty of the Game." He paused and, reaching under the blanket, withdrew a bottle. "Time for your medicine, ain't it?"

Heavy Pete grinned, too happy even to speak what with the superb Havana, the intelligent conversation of the Reverend which abounded with useful information, and the soon to be imbibed elixir. Miller Muldoon poured.

"You got to have seven players for it to work. Let's say I'm the dealer. I call for a brand-new deck. Thing is, if you use an old deck, then you have got to be sure the cards are arranged in numerical order, just the way they are when they come in the package—like, ace, deuce, trey, and so on, right up to the king."

Miller paused for a drink. He was enjoying himself. He loved to talk about the art of the Game. Nor had he any fear of giving away secrets, for the hand *is* quicker than the eye, and the dude *is* more gullible than a starving dog.

He resumed, his lips wet with the pleasures of the bottle and with the words that he had already spoken, as well as those for which he was preparing. "On account of a new deck is supposed to be thoroughly mixed up before you start to play, the dealer makes several fake shuffles. You see what I mean? Here." Miller took the deck and illustrated by letting all the cards in his right hand fall ahead of those in his left, then the other way around.

"Golly," said Heavy Pete O'Hay.

Miller Muldoon showed the maneuver again, but this time so fast that Pete couldn't see it was false. Heavy Pete's mouth fell open, dumb with awe, his eyes bleak with reverence.

"Actually, it's no different from a straight cut, except that the dealer pretends to shuffle the deck," Muldoon said. "Thing is to do it with the hands cupped—and you can pick a good time for it, I mean a time when the play is dull and so the others in the game are not so sharp." He paused, smiling benevolently at his student.

"After the shuffle and cut, you deal the first round from the top, in the regular manner, to all seven players. The next round is the same, except the dealer takes the bottom card. Remember, he knows what that card is. On the third round, he deals in the regular way again to all seven. The same for the fourth round, except the dealer again takes a card from the bottom."

Miller Muldoon paused to refresh himself with some elixir. "Now, the fifth is critical. The fifth round. Pay attention now! The first player on the dealer's left gets the top card in order." All the while, of course, Miller Muldoon was dealing the cards, illustrating to his student how he slipped a card from the bottom of the deck, and indeed went through all the moves of a real game.

"Now then, the dealer, using the thumb of his left hand—the hand holding the deck—slips back the top card far enough to let him deal the next card from beneath it. That's the second card down. He repeats this two more times, and then to the next man—that's the fifth, counting from his left—he slips the card he has been holding back with his thumb.

"The sixth man—the man on the dealer's right—gets his card in the regular order. Now the dealer slips himself the bottom card, and so seven hands have been dealt."

Miller Muldoon leaned back and surveyed the seven hands he had dealt out onto the horse blanket. He grinned at Heavy Pete's amazement. "You're a good pupil," he said. "You keep yer mouth shut."

Heavy Pete beamed with pleasure.

"Now then, pay close attention! The first player—he's on my immediate left—he'll find he has a pat full house and he'll make a pretty good bet to protect it, but not enough to scare anyone out of the game.

"The second, third, fourth, and fifth players will all have two pairs each, with an odd fifth card, so it's just enough to suck them in. You follow?"

Heavy Pete nodded in excitement. He could almost feel himself actually playing the game Muldoon was describing so graphically.

"The sixth player, who is on my immediate right, also discovers he has a full house. He'll call the opening bet and raise. Now then. The dealer looks at his own hand." Miller Muldoon did so in illustration, picking up his cards and perusing them carefully. "He has a pair and three other cards of one suit. These run consecutively, like the seven, eight, and nine of spades, say. He knows that on the bottom of the deck there will be the ten and jack of spades, which will make him a straight flush. But..." The Reverend held up his hand, palm facing Heavy Pete. "But he is not desirous of driving out the other players—that is to say, he doesn't want to lose their money—and so he only calls.

"The two pat full houses naturally don't take any cards from the draw, but the players with the pairs do. However, no matter what they draw, the four sets of two pairs can't be helped and will drop out when the betting stiffens. This will leave the dealer and the players with the two full houses."

The Reverend chuckled and drew another nip from his bottle, passing it to Heavy Pete, who did likewise. Both pulled on their cigars, savoring the moment as the Master approached the climax of the Lesson.

"The dealer's two cards from the bottom give him an unbeatable straight flush, and he can shoot his whole wad. But...!" And the Reverend held up his forefinger, rigid as a ruler. "He must bet conservatively until after the draw, because there is always the chance that somebody *might*..." and he said the word softly, ending with a wince, "somebody just might demand a cut." He paused for emphasis.

"At the same time, the dealer has to keep an eye on his last card, because if it happens to be a king or a queen he can't get a straight flush. Still, this happens maybe only once in a dozen hands or more, and if it happens, then he simply drops out, and all he loses is his ante. But if his last card happens to be an ace, he has to draw four cards, the deuce, trey, four, and five. Fortunately, the ace only shows itself about once in twenty or so deals."

The Reverend laid the deck of cards reverently down on the horse blanket and, leaning back, regarded his awestruck pupil.

"So then you bet the whole shebang," muttered Heavy Pete.

"You bet your ass, *and* your balls," replied the Reverend.

Miller Muldoon was pleased. As he told Slocum later, he found Heavy Pete O'Hay to be a sparkling conversationalist and a most intelligent man.

12

Each morning and evening Slocum rode out to scout the trail ahead, and he also checked the back trail. There was no sign of the LeForts. He had followed their old trail, which he and Dinwiddie had picked up by the creek, followed it until it staled out as they headed north. It seemed clear that they were leaving the country, at least for the time being. Of course, he realized it could have been a maneuver, and that they would circle back and follow the herd. He didn't mind; the point was that he kept a sharp lookout, with outriders posted within the perimeter of the moving KC herd.

"That's the deadline," he told his riders, showing them the distance that would be the periphery of the herd at any given time. "You see anything, anything at all, that looks suspicious inside that area, you let me know right now."

And so far there had been nothing. Thus, the herd with its guarded periphery moved north through Kansas.

"Begins to appear we're making Case's deadline," Dinwiddie observed.

"The LeForts will hit us, either here or in town. I'd say it'll be on the trail."

Dinwiddie nodded, canting his head, his good eye searching Slocum's tanned face. "I'd go with that. They don't want the cattle to get to the shipping point. Even if they do wipe us all out afterwards, the shippers

169

will see the cattle made it; and the cowmen, too."

Slocum took off his hat and ran his sleeved forearm across his forehead, then put his hat back on. "Just keep up your gun practice, old timer."

"Don't worry about that. These old bones are telling me it'll be tight from here on in."

It was noon now. The white disc of sun burned down on the men and animals as they moved slowly over the dry tawny-colored terrain, enveloped in a cloud of dust, the riders with their bandannas pulled over their faces in protection. They were tired, the men, not to mention the lone girl. They were all tired, but their spirits were high. They had come through something. Yet Slocum indefatigably snapped at them to remain on the alert.

"This drive ain't over yet. Remember that. Don't forget it for a minute. As long as there are two LeForts out there somewhere, we don't sleep. Remember that!"

Even so, thoughts turned to the pleasures at the end of the trail—the saloons, the cribs, the sounds of laughter and music and girls and camaraderie. Even Dinwiddie couldn't always keep his thoughts away from Nellie: thoughts of their spread when he got paid for the herd, thoughts of their life together, mental images of her body.

Slocum knew that Gans and Porky were waiting for just this: for the men to soften, to lower their guard, their vigilance. He snapped at them harder than ever.

Meanwhile, in the evenings, Ava came to him; though occasionally not. And he didn't mind that. He knew she had to keep things right with Muldoon. That was her business. His business, as far as she was concerned, was only when they were together. But as they moved closer to their destination he was reluctant to lose himself even for an hour or two, as he invariably did when they were together thrashing around in his bedroll.

One time he told her they'd have to wait until later, until things were settled with the LeForts or they reached Abilene. She understood, smiling up at him as they stood in the trees along the side of a creek one late afternoon.

"Then get that business settled quickly, please, Mr. Slocum. This lady finds that whatever you have been doing with her has destroyed any possibility of her ever wanting to do anything else anywhere or any time, ever."

"I'll do my best, Mrs. Muldoon."

She had held his steady gaze then, each of them looking deeply into the other's eyes.

Then she said, "If I might use the words of a famous man, Mr. Slocum..." and she was imitating his voice and manner of speaking to the men. "I don't want you to do your best. I want you to do it!"

He awakened all at once with the tang of danger in his nostrils, in his eyes. It was still dark—around midnight, he judged—as he sat bolt upright, his .31 in his hand.

A horse in the remuda had whinnied, and another followed, Slocum catching the fear in their sound. Now a steer bellowed and others began to follow from the creek where the herd had bedded down.

Instantly, the entire camp was awake, the men pulling on their boots over swollen feet, strapping on their gunbelts, throwing blanket and saddle on their ponies.

There was no need for anyone to say the word, but somebody did. It fell into the camp like a clap of thunder.

"Fire!"

Mounting swiftly, they saw the blaze across the creek, sweeping wide as it came toward the herd, which was on its feet, milling, roaring, and bawling, ready to stampede in any direction.

When Slocum got there the animals had already started to run ahead of the advancing flames, which were leaping high in the night, illuminating the whole of the countryside.

He was riding the spotted pony, barking orders to the men, some of whom he sent to head off the leaders, who were about to break into a charge.

The men jumped to his commands, the older ones anticipating what he intended, the younger simply following this man who always seemed to know something they didn't. By now they would have followed him into hell.

Right now, at this moment, the land *was* a hell— a blazing, crackling, roaring inferno of blasting, scorching heat and fear-crazed cattle and horses.

Now he ordered two of the men to kill one of the largest animals and split the carcass.

"Pair off!" he told the men. "Throw your rope on the hind legs, then drag him over to that big blaze yonder."

They did as they were told, shooting one of the bigger animals and splitting its carcass.

At a place where the fire was burning in an arroyo, where the blue-stem grass was tall, Slocum ordered that it be allowed to burn its way to a flat covered with shorter buffalo grass.

"Straddle the blaze!" he shouted, ordering the pair of cowboys, one on the burnt side, right up close, and the other so that he was riding in the path of the smoke with his rope played all the way out to its bite on his saddlehorn.

"You drag that wet carcass slowly along the line of the fire. I mean slow!"

And he watched that they did it right, until the carcass was worn to ribbons.

Even before then he had ordered another animal killed and its carcass split.

"Drag that one now!"

In the meantime, Dinwiddie had the men thrashing out isolated spots of the fire, using pieces of wet cowhide or wet saddle blankets.

In this manner they fought the fire, working all night and through the next morning, eating hastily broiled beef in snatches, without time even for coffee, for they ate in the saddle. It wasn't until the following afternoon that the fire was beaten.

As they sat exhausted by the chuck wagon drinking Ava's coffee, their lungs filled with smoke, some of the men with their hair and clothing singed, Miller Muldoon took on the role that everyone knew was not rightfully his, but which they now accepted because of the need.

He read from the book of prayer which he had purchased along with the wagon. Eager hands unloaded the organ and Ava played while they all sang. It was a good moment, was the way Heavy Pete summed it up.

Dinwiddie had a different comment to make as he and Slocum stood by the rope corral the horse wrangler had thrown up for the remuda.

"You wondering what I'm wondering, Slocum?"

"I am not wondering it," Slocum said.

"Gans and Porky, huh."

Slocum nodded. "There are horseshoe tracks yonder where the fire started. Two horses. Fresh prints. One of the horses had a loose shoe, the same as what we saw when we cut their trail down by that creek a while back."

"You got a notion then why they didn't start shooting at us when we were all busy and they had the chance?"

"One good reason might be they didn't want us to know it was them started the fire. Though they were sure careless. The other might be they're running out of ammunition."

In the early time before the dawn, Otis Dinwiddie awakened from a dream of Nellie. He sat up on his bedroll feeling the cool morning on his hands and face. Then, being a true cowman, he first put on his hat, then his pants and boots.

It was his morning to scout the eastern periphery, while Slocum took the west. The sorrel he'd been riding the day before had shown a hint of oncoming lameness, so he roped the buckskin, deciding to let the big red horse rest till he examined him more closely when it was daylight. Buck went through his usual routine of swelling his belly, trying to bite his rider, and even crowhopping; then he settled.

As Dinwiddie rode out of the camp the tip of the sun was just showing at the horizon. He was wide awake now, clearing his nose and throat, spitting, settling into his saddle. He wore a brace of sixguns, for he was still not sure of his right hand, which now and again still stiffened. He flexed it now in the cool air—and, yes, it wasn't as limber as he would have liked. Well, he reasoned—yet again—maybe between the two hands, if the moment came for a call-out, maybe he'd manage. A dour reflection.

When he reached the creek at the limit of his swing east, and hadn't seen anything unusual, he dismounted and, kneeling at the edge of the water, drank. Rising, he remembered the long fingernail that had caught in his belt the day before when he'd drawn his gun in practice. Drawing his skinning knife from its sheath at his waist, he pared the nail and, while he was about it, pared the other nine as well. Then he tested the sharp blade on his callused thumb and slipped the knife back into its sheath.

The sun was up now, its light shining through the trees along the creek bank as he moved away from the water, unbuttoning his fly as he did so. He was looking forward to his morning coffee as he stood there urinating.

"Drop your gunbelt, Dinwiddie!"

The voice came hard and cold from directly behind him. Dinwiddie was surprised to find that he could keep on urinating as with his left hand he unbuckled and let his two sixguns and belt fall down around his feet. He buttoned up then, making sure that his mackinaw covered the sheath knife.

"Turn around—slowly. Your hands up high!"

"Can't put my left any higher. I got lead in the shoulder."

As he turned, his eyes took in more than Porky LeFort standing there with a sawed-off shotgun pointed right at his guts. He saw the saddle horse tied to one of the willows, allowing his eyes, without leaving the man in front of him, to take in a wide terrain.

"Surprised, huh!" Porky's triumph was all over his big face. "I was going to shoot you when you had yer whanger out, but I want you to know who it is blowing you to hell, you son of a bitch."

"That goose gun'll do the job good enough, Porky. But that's just murdering me. Why don't we fight it out even-like. See who's the better man?"

"I already know who's the better man. But you filled my daddy with that load of blue whistlers, you son of a bitch, and I am going to pay you back the same. You get it? I bin saving this load. Kept it in this here Greener all this time. A special load just for you, Dinwiddie. For Daddy."

"And you got Gans backing you, right?"

A hard chuckle fell from Porky's wet lips, but Dinwiddie saw that he had scored.

"Can't do much without Gans, can you? None of you boys ever could wipe your own ass or ears without Gans."

"Dinwiddie, this is you and me. Gans wanted to wait, but I—me, Porky—decided to get you right now. Gans can have Slocum. But you—you're my meat. And Daddy's!"

"You'll never make it out of here, Porky. We've got double guard on the whole herd. Swing is covered with two men on each side, plus the point and drag. They'll hear that blast and they'll be right on your ass. I mean right now."

"I know about your double guard, Dinwiddie. I bin laying for you. Watching."

"That's what I know. We've all been expecting you."

"You weren't expecting me when you were taking that leak a minute ago." And big Porky chuckled at his score.

Dinwiddie, cold inside at the truth of Porky's observation, said nothing.

"Too much talkin'," Porky said, though he was clearly enjoying himself. "So get on that horse." He had, meanwhile, reached behind him to take the reins of his own saddle horse. One-handed, he undid the reins that had been wrapped but not tied around a branch of a willow.

"You climb on your horse," Porky said. "And remember—one false move and I will cut you right off at yer balls."

"Where are we going?" Dinwiddie asked, trying to run up some time. "Going to see Gans? Going to go and brag it to Gans?"

"You ain't getting me mad with that talk, mister. Gans has got nothing to do with this. I believe I told you, it's you and me." Which was what Dinwiddie wanted to know. With his eyes never leaving Dinwiddie, Porky took the reins in his left hand and grabbed a handful of his horse's mane, still holding the sawed-off shotgun in his right, with its deadly muzzles pointed right at Dinwiddie, who was already in his saddle.

"Gentle that horse of yours!" Porky's words came sharp as the buckskin swung his head back to take a nip at Dinwiddie's leg.

Dinwiddie knew Buck's tricks; he'd tried them on every one of the KC riders. But he was a top cow pony, full of piss and vinegar. And right now that was exactly what Dinwiddie wanted, as he watched Buck's ears lying flat back down along his neck. He knew he was mad, having kneed him as hard as he could when he climbed into the saddle.

He had brushed aside the edge of his mackinaw so that his hand, which was out of Porky's view, lay right against the handle of his skinning knife. Buck was still spooking, and now, at a leg pressure from his rider, he spun just as Porky started to mount his horse. At that precise moment, when Porky had his foot in the stirrup, Dinwiddie drew the knife and stuck its point right into Buck's side. Buck let out a scream of rage and lashed out with both rear hooves. At the same time, Dinwiddie dove across his withers, rolling to cover by a clump of young willows. He heard Porky scream, and when he came up on his knees on the ground, he saw Buck kicking and bucking around in a circle, trying to get his saddle off. And Porky LeFort was lying on the ground motionless.

Dinwiddie waited. One mistake had been enough today. Finally the buckskin calmed down and shook his head, snorting, and then began cropping some of the grass nearby. Dinwiddie continued to listen. He heard nothing. At length, satisfied that Porky had been telling the truth and that he was alone, he stood up and walked carefully to where his gunbelt was lying. Only when he had strapped it on and saw that his weapons were all right did he take a closer look at the motionless LeFort. Porky's neck was broken, his face smashed. He was dead.

Dinwiddie raised his head and looked at the buckskin serenely cropping the grass only a few feet away. Then he walked over and gathered his reins and came back to the dead man. He removed the gun and cartridge belt and picked up the wicked scattergun. Then he mounted Buck and rode back to camp.

13

It was the last day of April when the KC herd hit Abilene to one of the biggest celebrations even the old timers had ever seen.

The festivities consisted of a parade, speeches, half a dozen dances, fistfights, sexual encounters, laughter, tears, rage, and joy, including half a dozen accidents and one intentional though drunken killing. Among a minority of the citizenry, a good bit of head-wagging took place, with dire predictions of the town's future with it now being open to the cattle trade. But the merchants were overjoyed. The festivities lasted all night and into the following morning. Eli Case was beside himself with joy. And Otis Dinwiddie was not outdistanced by the little cattle dealer.

"Slocum, we have made history!" Case kept saying over and over amidst the din of firecrackers, a brass band, shouts and screams, the neighing of horses and the bawling of cattle, along with the fireworks from six-shooters and other weapons.

Dinwiddie, tapping his pocket where he had his money, kept saying how he was going to climb aboard his Nellie and ride her till by God she bucked him off: "... and I'll by God dast her to do it!"

Slocum was enjoying himself, relieved that the job was over, pleased with his thousand dollars from Case, who threw in a little extra in case he ever needed to call on John Slocum again.

"It's all over but the shouting!" Eli Case kept saying.

But Slocum knew it wasn't. There was still Gans LeFort. And it was funny, he thought. Funny how it was Miller Muldoon who'd killed Dutch Dillman, and Dinwiddie who'd taken care of Porky. He, Slocum, had somehow not been slated for those confrontations. It gave him a kind of strange feeling of being left out, he decided ruefully. But there was still Gans. No, it sure wasn't over.

"See," Dinwiddie said as they leaned on the bar in the Suddenly Riches Saloon, "see, all that practicing with my left hand and all, and them bottles—shit, I didn't need it. Not that it wasn't useful, I am saying."

"But you did need it," Slocum said, and his tone was insistent. "No, you didn't get to pull your trigger. But that practicing is what sharpened you for what you did do. Make no mistake, my friend."

Dinwiddie looked him right in the eye now and said, "You are right, friend. I'll drink to you on that, John Slocum!"

Later, as Slocum and Ava lay in bed in his room at the Trail House, she said, "Where will you go now?"

"Wind River country."

"What's there?"

"Everything."

"Miller wants to head for Denver."

"Good gambling country, Denver. You taking the organ and prayer books?"

She smiled, nestling in his bare arms. "Nope. But I wish you'd come along. We'd make a good threesome."

"Haven't you ever heard that three's a crowd?"

"Miller doesn't mind. I told you he's always been good to me."

"Thanks. But I don't need him to be good to me."

He knew it was their last time and it was good because it was clean.

"I'll not forget you, John Slocum," she said.

"Good enough."

"Don't you want to ask me to come along with you to the Wind River country?"

He stood up and began putting on his clothes and didn't answer her. She waited a moment and then started dressing. When they were downstairs and out in the street she said again, "Don't you want to ask me to come along with you to the Wind River country?"

"Don't spoil it," Slocum said. And he kissed her on the tip of her nose as the stage from Libertyville drove down and a couple of young passengers hooted at them.

She looked up into his green eyes. "Thank you. Thank you for reminding me. I almost forgot." And she turned and walked quickly away.

As he started in the other direction he saw the stage stopping outside the express office and the passengers alighting.

Walking down to the Suddenly Riches Saloon, he was glad she had left. Not that he didn't want her; but it would be a hell of a note having her in the way now after all they'd been through.

When he walked into the Suddenly Riches Saloon, the first person Slocum saw was Otis Dinwiddie. The cattleman was having a snootful, regaling some of his trail crew and a few hangers-on with stories of "the good old days; may they never come back!" This line brought a laugh each time he said it, which was frequently.

"You drinking up your money instead of getting home to Nellie?" Slocum asked.

Dinwiddie grinned. "Nope. I got it all set. I'm pulling out in the morning. You want to come along?"

Slocum shook his head as he picked up the bottle and, looking at two of the KC riders, said, "No, but I want to talk to you three gents in the back room there for a minute."

Without waiting for an answer he walked across the floor and opened the door next to the end of the bar. Dinwiddie and the two KC hands came right in after him.

"What's up?" Dinwiddie wanted to know, and when Slocum stood the bottle on the table and told them all to sit down, the cattleman started to splutter.

Slocum turned to the two other men who had ridden with the herd all the way from Texas. "I don't have time to explain. But Dinwiddie there's enjoying his relaxing after that long ride. There is going to be trouble in the next room in a minute or two, and I want you to keep him in here. You got it?" He eyed each of them in turn. "I'll come and tell you when to bring him out. You mind that, now!"

Dinwiddie started to expostulate, but his hand was reaching for the bottle of whiskey and by the time he'd poured and taken a swallow Slocum was gone, locking the door behind him.

At the bar Slocum nodded to the man on the sober side and said, "Don't let anybody in that room there."

"Who the hell are you, mister?" And then, taking a second look, the man behind the bar started over. "Right. Right, I got 'cha."

Slocum stood at the bar now and watched some of

the heads turning in his direction, but nobody came up to speak. He could hear no commotion coming from the back room and so he assumed Dinwiddie and his men were addressing the bottle he had left them.

He didn't have to wait long. The bartender had placed a glass and bottle in front of him and had wiped down the mahogany bar for the third time when the batwing doors swung wide open and the big man came in.

And the room stopped.

"You—Slocum!"

Slocum was standing with his back to the room, but with a clear view of everything behind him through the big gilt-framed mirror. Gans LeFort had stopped only a few feet away. He was wearing two sixguns in tied-down holsters.

Slocum turned slowly to face him.

"Where is Dinwiddie?"

"You'll have to get past me first, LeFort."

"I am aiming to do that, Slocum. And then I am going to kill that other son of a bitch."

"How?" He was standing loose, yet with that precise relaxation and attention that was missing nothing. He had already loosed the hammer thong on the Colt.

"A bullet's too easy," Gans said. "I'd planned to blow your guts out, but now I'm going to carve you. I'm going to carve you with my pigsticker. A bullet's too quick." Holding his eyes on Slocum, he bent forward a little to untie the rawhide around his legs that was holding down his holsters. "I'll drop these guns."

And it was in that precision of his watching and listening that Slocum caught it. Gans was talking too much. And as the big man moved, Slocum was feeling his every move inside his own self, in his own body;

even knowing what Gans LeFort was thinking.

And so Slocum struck for his gun at the exact moment that Gans's hand swept to the hideout in his shoulder holster.

"I'd been expecting you," Slocum said as Gans sank to the floor of the Suddenly Riches Saloon with the neat, round hole between his eyes.

It was just as he dropped the Colt back into its holster that Slocum knew he'd made his mistake. He was already diving for the floor as the shot crashed into the room, the bullet driving a big chip out of the bar exactly where he had been standing an instant before.

He was rolling across the floor now, and dove behind the bar as two more bullets cut into the mahogany and a third smashed the big mirror.

In the next moment of silence the man with the gun spoke. "Slocum, come on out, you come on out of there. I am going to kill you!"

Looking up into the mirror, Slocum almost dropped his gun. For it was Gans LeFort standing there; it was Gans LeFort, whom he'd just shot and killed, standing there with the big hogleg in his hand covering the top of the long bar and its sides.

"Slocum, you don't have a chance. I'll stay here till you starve to death."

And then Slocum caught it.

"I didn't know Gans had a *twin*."

"Shit, you do now; exceptin' it is not Gans who's got the twin, it's Goose has the twin. Goose LeFort. I see I got here late; but I am going to make up for it. Slocum!"

There was no way out. No one in the room was moving. And he knew, too, that Goose had the door covered from where he was standing, as well as the entire bar.

Another shot rang out, smashing the mirror again, and another shot hit the bartender's cash box, which was on the shelf in back of the bar and just above Slocum's head. The shelf had a leg right under the cash box, supporting it from the floor. Slocum grabbed it. Sometimes... And he pulled as another shot rang out and the box came tumbling down on top of him.

"Slocum!"

And he was in luck. Sometimes, he knew, bartenders kept a gun in the box, insurance against unruly customers. The gun was a derringer, but it would serve his purpose. He had already spotted the ball of string on the shelf beneath the bar and in a moment he had tied one end around the derringer's trigger, first having made sure the gun was loaded. He had a pretty good idea of where Goose was located, but because of the broken mirror and the fact that he was lying on the floor Slocum couldn't actually see him.

The plan was simple. Quickly he crawled down to one end of the bar and braced the derringer with two boxes of empty bottles so that it lay on its side, held between the two boxes. He crawled back to the other end of the bar, paying out the string. He checked his Colt, saw that the string was taut, and waited. But there was only silence. No one in the room seemed even to be breathing.

He crawled back to the other end of the bar by the derringer.

"Go fuck yourself, LeFort!" he called out, and instantly crawled back to the other end again as the shot rang out, giving him an idea of Goose's placement. But he knew the voice alone wouldn't fool

LeFort. This time he called from where he was and as Goose fired at the new location, he pulled the string to fire the derringer at the other end. At the same moment he was on his feet and in the second when Goose's attention was taken between the voice and the sound of the derringer, Slocum shot him dead from the middle of the bar.

It was some moments before a thin voice in the frozen crowd said, "He is dead."

Nobody argued it.

As men came forward to remove the two bodies, Slocum poured himself a drink. He downed it and turned back to face the room. Raising his glass again, his eyes caught the blond girl up on the balcony. He couldn't remember her name. Sally? Callie?

He heard the hammering at the door of the back room where he had left Dinwiddie and the two KC men. Without turning around and with his eyes still on the girl who was smiling down at him, he dropped the key onto the bar behind him and picked up the bottle of whiskey.

As he started toward the stairs he was thinking: *Why not? Wasn't this where he came in?*

GREAT WESTERN YARNS FROM ONE OF THE BEST-SELLING WRITERS IN THE FIELD TODAY

JAKE LOGAN

___ 06551-0	LAW COMES TO COLD RAIN	$2.25
___ 07395-5	ACROSS THE RIO GRANDE	$2.50
___ 0-867-21003	BLOODY TRAIL TO TEXAS	$1.95
___ 0-867-21041	THE COMANCHE'S WOMAN	$1.95
___ 0-872-16979	OUTLAW BLOOD	$1.95
___ 06191-4	THE CANYON BUNCH	$2.25
___ 05956-1	SHOTGUNS FROM HELL	$2.25
___ 06132-9	SILVER CITY SHOOTOUT	$2.25
___ 07398-X	SLOCUM AND THE LAW	$2.50
___ 06255-4	SLOCUM'S JUSTICE	$2.25
___ 05958-8	SLOCUM'S RAID	$1.95
___ 06481-6	SWAMP FOXES	$2.25
___ 0-872-16823	SLOCUM'S CODE	$1.95
___ 06532-4	SLOCUM'S COMMAND	$2.25
___ 0-867-21071	SLOCUM'S DEBT	$1.95
___ 0-425-05998-7	SLOCUM'S DRIVE	$2.25
___ 0-867-21090	SLOCUM'S GOLD	$1.95
___ 0-867-21023	SLOCUM'S HELL	$1.95

JAKE LOGAN

___ 0-867-21087	SLOCUM'S REVENGE	$1.95
___ 07296-3	THE JACKSON HOLE TROUBLE	$2.50
___ 07182-0	SLOCUM AND THE CATTLE QUEEN	$2.75
___ 06413-1	SLOCUM GETS EVEN	$2.50
___ 06744-0	SLOCUM AND THE LOST DUTCHMAN MINE	$2.50
___ 07018-2	BANDIT GOLD	$2.50
___ 06846-3	GUNS OF THE SOUTH PASS	$2.50
___ 07046-8	SLOCUM AND THE HATCHET MEN	$2.50
___ 07258-4	DALLAS MADAM	$2.50
___ 07139-1	SOUTH OF THE BORDER	$2.50
___ 07460-9	SLOCUM'S CRIME	$2.50
___ 07567-2	SLOCUM'S PRIDE	$2.50
___ 07382-3	SLOCUM AND THE GUN-RUNNERS	$2.50
___ 07494-3	SLOCUM'S WINNING HAND	$2.50
___ 08382-9	SLOCUM IN DEADWOOD	$2.50

Prices may be slightly higher in Canada.

Available at your local bookstore or return this form to:

BERKLEY
Book Mailing Service
P.O. Box 690, Rockville Centre, NY 11571

Please send me the titles checked above. I enclose _____. Include 75¢ for postage and handling if one book is ordered; 25¢ per book for two or more not to exceed $1.75. California, Illinois, New York and Tennessee residents please add sales tax.

NAME_____

ADDRESS_____

CITY_____ STATE/ZIP_____

(allow six weeks for delivery)

162b